Studies in Romance Languages ⸝2

Machado de Assis

The Hand & the Glove

Translated by ALBERT I. BAGBY, Jr.

with a Foreword by Helen Caldwell

The University Press of Kentucky

Standard Book Number: 8131–1211–7

Library of Congress Catalog Card Number 74–111502

Copyright © 1970 by The University Press of Kentucky

A statewide cooperative scholarly publishing agency
serving Berea College, Centre College of Kentucky,
Eastern Kentucky University, Kentucky State College,
Morehead State University, Murray State University,
University of Kentucky, University of Louisville,
and Western Kentucky University.

Editorial and Sales Offices: Lexington, Kentucky 40506

Foreword

For a long time it has been the custom to call Machado de Assis
a pessimist. Here, however, in *The Hand and the Glove*, Mr.
Bagby presents to us the Brazilian master's indubitably comic
novel with its indubitably happy ending, *A Mão e a Luva*.

A Mão e a Luva is a romantic comedy, even though it pokes
fun at romance, at the romantic movement, and at the romantic
hero whether he be out of Goethe or out of Stendhal. In this,
Assis' second novel, we do not find the mature artist of his
"great" novels. We do find a hint of what is to come. The young
novelist is already experimenting with a narrative art which he
would transform into a full-toned instrument in those later
works. The character Guiomar—proud, womanly, by turns affectionate and coldly aloof—gives promise of that strange, wonder-
ful Capitú, *Dom Casmurro's* heroine. And throughout there
plays the lively wit that is Machado de Assis.

English-speaking readers who are already acquainted with
Machado de Assis will welcome this latest addition to the translated novels. True, it is a period piece; but its quaintness is a
charm to carry us back to the Rio de Janeiro of the 1850s—to
vanished courtly elegance and attitudes. *A Mão e a Luva* has also
the charm of being Machado de Assis at his most light-hearted,
his most ebullient—a charm that the later Machado de Assis was
loath to tamper with. In his foreword to the 1907 edition, he
wrote: "The thirty-odd years that separate the appearance of this
little novel from its present reissue explain the differences in
composition and in the temper of the author. If he would not
write the story in this way today, it is certain that this is the way
he wrote it back in those days. . . . He has altered
nothing. . . ."

The following year, with *all* his novels behind him, the old

Assis still found pleasure in this work of his younger self. In July 1908 he wrote his friend Mário de Alencar, "Today, during the day, I reread *A Mão e a Luva.*" Now, we too can know what drew the old novelist back to this early tale, for *The Hand and the Glove* recreates in English the elegant background, the charming heroine, the comedy, and the light-hearted ebullience of the Portuguese original.

HELEN CALDWELL

Introduction

Joaquim Maria Machado de Assis was born on June 21, 1839, in a poor neighborhood of Rio de Janeiro called the Morro do Livramento. He was a *mestiço,* which in Brazil means "of mixed blood." His father, Francisco José de Assis, was a mulatto and his mother, Maria Leopoldina Machado, a washerwoman of Portuguese extraction. In 1849, Machado's mother died of tuberculosis, and it is now known that his father remarried—a mulatto, Maria Inés—in 1854.[1] Thus it was that Assis received his first real teaching and training from his stepmother.

The boy's childhood was spent in that area of Rio in which he was born. He received his elementary education in a public school, and even at an early age manifested an interest in a literary career. His father, who was a painter, preferred that the boy elect a more practical, financially advantageous occupation, and so he went to work for a paper company. But his wandering mind and his interest in books made him leisurely about his work. Because of the family's financial difficulties, the boy also was forced to sell homemade candies to help provide a livelihood.

Then he met Madame Gallot, a bakery owner who taught him French. During this time he worked for the Paula Brito Bookstore, where his literary ambitions at last found opportunity for development. His first work, published there in 1855, was the poem "Ela" ("She").

In 1856 he went to work as a typesetter's apprentice for the Tipografia Nacional, today known as the Imprensa Nacional. Once again his literary interests and preoccupations made him a slow worker, but the director tolerated his failings in one area in order to encourage his interest in matters which were more to the liking of his spirit. After two years there, he began work on the

Correio Mercantil where, as an assistant and reviewer, he began to climb out of obscurity, exercising his talents in poetry and the theater. From 1860 to 1867 he worked for the *Diário do Rio de Janeiro,* and from 1867 to 1875 collaborated with the *Semana Ilustrada.* The young man's sincere dedication to serious intellectual work moved him well along toward the career which he had long envisioned. His financial lot improved considerably during this period and his various publications, though saturated with romanticism, made him known in literary and artistic circles. His first volume of poetry, *Crisálidas,* was published in 1864 and Assis' talents during this period were spread among poetry, theater, and journalism.

Assis' life to this point had been one so completely given to the demanding task of accomplishing his literary ambitions that aside from an occasional and inconsequential flirtation, he had not found the time in his busy schedule to pursue leisurely or romantic interests. The Assis of these years was almost entirely a coldly intellectual man.

But, in the year 1867, at the age of twenty-eight, he met Carolina Xavier de Novais, a refined, mature and attractive young Portuguese woman who had just arrived in Brazil. Assis met her apparently through her brother, Faustino Xavier de Novais, his friend and a Portuguese poet. He seemed to find in this woman, descended from the aristocracy, a tender understanding spirit that suited his desire for social and intellectual prominence, a woman whose love for and dedication to him and whose appreciation of his work would serve as a complement to his life. The marriage was of course strongly opposed by Carolina's other brothers on racial grounds, but with the determination of Carolina and the support of Faustino, the couple was married on November 12, 1869.

Thus began a period of conjugal happiness and productivity which lasted some thirty-five years. Initial financial obstacles

[1] Some writers have claimed—erroneously—that Francisco died in 1851. See, however, Luiz Viana Filho, *A Vida de Machado de Assis* (São Paulo: Livraria Martins Editora, 1965), pp. 11–18.

were overcome as Assis moved into maturity and literary fame with the publication of his first two romances, *Ressurreição* and *A Mão e a Luva*, in 1872 and 1874 respectively. His appointment to the position of first officer of the State Secretariat of the Ministry of Agriculture, Commerce, and Public Works in 1873 gave him an income that permitted him to further his writing. But the pressures of his job at the Secretariat, added to his efforts at completing *Iaiá Garcia* in 1878, necessitated a rest, and he took a leave from his post at the Secretariat. Accompanying his physical exhaustion were worsening attacks of epilepsy which, along with various intestinal disorders, he had long suffered from.

In the mountains of the state of Rio, Carolina became at once a wife, a mother, and a nurse to the convalescing Machado. Without doubt, these four months in Friburgo—one of the rare occasions on which Assis left the city of Rio—gave the author a different and more mature perspective of life which was reflected almost immediately thereafter in his writing.

With his return to Rio began the richest period of his literary production. The novel *Memórias Póstumas de Braz Cubas,* published in volume form in 1881, inaugurated this new period in his life; following close after it came two other novels of the first order, *Quincas Borba* and *Dom Casmurro.* He was now famous.

But Assis continued to be plagued and embarrassed by his epileptic condition, and myopia kept him temporarily away from his work. Determined nevertheless to achieve success in all his strivings, he excelled equally in his civil duties and in 1889 was promoted to director of the Directory of Commerce in the Ministry of Agriculture.

Basically Machado de Assis was a reserved and introverted personality. Despite his earnest determination to triumph over his strong feelings of inferiority, he was nonetheless affected visibly by the frustrations which life and circumstance had brought him. He continued to be extremely sensitive about his epileptic fits and his racial heritage (the latter, especially, was a matter of concern in the intellectual circles in which Assis moved). Added to these were myopia and an impediment in speech. It is perhaps for these reasons that, despite his shyness, he sought out a life of association, attempting to forget these disabilities by mingling with groups where he was respected and appreciated openly. Among the clubs he belonged to were the Association of Brazilian Men of Letters (1883) and the Society of Letters and Arts (1887). As a crowning accomplishment to his desire to see born an organization which would provide order and prestige to the literary life of Rio, he was the first president of the Brazilian Academy of Letters, and remained in that office until his death.

The prestige and fame of the humble *mestiço* of the Livramento was now established; he had become the glory of Brazil. But his time was waning. Carolina, his devoted wife, became seriously ill and a trip to Friburgo for recuperation was in vain. When she died on October 20, 1904, Machado de Assis, profoundly feeling the loss of his strength and companion, began his own slow decline. His last novel, the short work *Memorial de Aires,* published in 1908, is Assis' recollection of the memories of his dear wife. The pessimism which many a critic has noted and will insist is a mainstay of his works is not present in this novelette, though its tone is one of sadness and melancholy.

Machado de Assis died on September 29, 1908, surrounded by some of his closest friends and highest representatives of Brazilian letters—José Veríssimo, Euclides da Cunha, and Coelho Neto—and knowing the heritage which he himself had left behind was enduring and everlasting. Already one of the highest expressions of Brazilian literary achievement, he would become a few years later one of the most important literary figures of his hemisphere as his works were translated into German, French, and Spanish.

Machado de Assis is often regarded by critics as Brazil's most outstanding writer of prose fiction. Fiction was not the only vehicle for Assis' literary expression, however; he tried his hand at nearly all of them—theater, poetry, and criticism as well. But it was in the novel and in his short stories that he managed to soar to universal heights. While it is seldom valid critical practice to apply superlatives to any author or work of art, the case of Machado de Assis might be considered a justifiable exception. Even a Henry James, says North American critic Samuel Putnam in *Marvelous Journey,* lacks the *sabedoria*—the great, deep, life wisdom—of Assis.[2]

The reader who is well acquainted with his novels, or *romances* as they are called, is able to appreciate what is meant by this wisdom. In delineation of character, Assis is probably unequaled by any writer in the Americas for incisiveness and perception. Through his use of metaphor and symbol and an exquisite manipulation of the language, he is able to penetrate deep into the soul of his characters. And it is by his keen description of their souls that we are likely to remember Assis' characters, for in them he lays bare the darkest regions of Everyman. Not that the physical description of people is neglected by the author; it is there also, but merely as a means by which the reader may be quickly transported into the inner labyrinths of the person's nature. How does Assis accomplish this? By using physical attributes, attitudes, conversation to direct the attention to what lies beneath the dress. Why is he able to do this? Perhaps because he is able to put something of himself into each of his characters.

Machado de Assis has generally been regarded as a romanticist who became a realist. Among the various literary genres which he cultivated, with different degrees of success, his novels —nine in number—are his highest achievement. *A Mão e a Luva* was his second novel chronologically and belongs to the period of romanticism, as do *Ressurreição* (his first effort), *Helena,* and *Iaiá Garcia.* These four novels were all written between the years 1872 and 1878. His realistic period is normally considered to begin with *Memórias Póstumas de Braz Cubas,* followed chronologically by *Quincas Borba, Dom Casmurro, Esaú e Jacó* and finally, the novelette *Memorial de Aires.*

[2] *Marvelous Journey: A Survey of Four Centuries of Brazilian Writing* (New York: Alfred A. Knopf, 1948), p. 183.

Despite the lines drawn here between his romantic and realistic writing, one should be constantly aware in reading Assis that these distinctions are merely guidelines; one could as easily say that the earlier novels were only steppingstones on the path to a maturer realism. The attempt to categorize an author of the caliber of Assis within such movements as romanticism, realism, or naturalism—the literary movements in vogue in his time—is dangerous. Like any truly universal author, Assis transcends movements. A man of his time to the extent that he follows along the edge of them all, borrowing from each the elements he needed, he is still neither a true romanticist nor a true realist or naturalist.

Assis is a writer and man of his day only in the restricted sense that much of his day is a part of his writing, but he is not imprisoned by his day or its aesthetics. Two outstanding elements of his works, his irony and humor, are *machadiano* in character; the irony never descends to the aggressive, mocking kind, nor does his humor reach to heights of spontaneous, resounding laughter. He is reserved, balanced in his romantic aspects, not falsifying or exaggerating his characters. In fact, the careful reader of *The Hand and the Glove* will note the author's approach to a satire of romanticism.

Further, Assis is an intelligent writer, subtle and profound, and as he explores the dark tunnels of life and the human soul he brings us an approach to life which is pensive, monolithic. Times past—events which have already occurred—are the means by which all that is significant in life is to be had, known, felt. And the best means to recapture all that has been or is, is through memories and recollections. This reflective kind of man and his writing belong neither to romanticism nor realism. Massaud Moisés, reluctant to classify the author, accedes to calling him a pre-Symbolist, Proustian in his evocation of memory to discover the meaning of the past and present.[3]

[3] Machado de Assis, *Ressurreição e A Mão e a Luva,* ed. Massaud Moisés (São Paulo: Editora Cultrix, 1968), intro., p. 20.

In the introduction to his translation of *Memórias Póstumas de Braz Cubas*, William Grossman depicts Machado de Assis as the most thoroughly disenchanted writer in occidental literature.[4]

Of the more than twenty books and innumerable articles and essays that have been written about Assis, the vast majority have dealt with the author's pessimism and classic taste in a period when romanticism prevailed. It is not an exaggeration to state that Assis saw with somber eyes; in fact, this is a mild remark indeed, considering the bitter, disillusioned, disheartening, and failing world which most critics have found to be the substance of Assis' artistic creation. Herminio Conde has stated that Assis was "un genio cuyo genio se afirmaba con un sentimiento amargo y áspero." [5]

We might attempt to explain the author's pessimism genetically—that is, to conclude that his somber artistic world was the inevitable result of the somber inner reality of an undersized, myopic, rachitic, epileptic son of a poor mulatto. Or, we might explain it by saying that his was a type of artistic bent that conceives of literary merit as a by-product of tragic characterizations and outcomes. But whatever reason we give for Assis' bleak outlook, the fact remains that his work has never been pictured outside of a pessimistic framework.

Grossman, an articulate spokesman for the majority, suggests that the reader has but two alternatives in confronting Assis: either to reject the author's view of life, or to reject the world.[6] What may seem on the surface exasperating to the casual reader of this author is his iconoclasm in which, seemingly, he rejects everything worldly.

It has been the general consensus that somber pessimism is the common denominator of all of Assis' nine novels. Three of

---

[4] Machado de Assis, *Epitaph of a Small Winner*, trans. William L. Grossman (New York: Noonday Press, 1952), p. 11.

[5] "A genius whose genius asserted itself with a bitter and harsh sentiment." *La Tragedia Ocular de Machado de Assis* (Buenos Aires: El Ateneo, 1947), p. 109.

[6] Assis, *Epitaph of a Small Winner*, p. 11.

these are generally regarded as masterpieces, and it is in the chronological trilogy of *Memórias Póstumas de Braz Cubas, Quincas Borba,* and *Dom Casmurro* that critics have been able to find the most convincing evidence to support their claims for Machado's disenchantment.

Samuel Putnam has been able to find only one character among Assis' creations whom he considers wholly endowed with goodness and virtue—Rubião, in *Quincas Borba,* whose reward for his goodness is insanity: [7] innocence cruelly punished, it could be said. But even Rubião is not really innocent of egoism, a characteristic to be found to a greater or lesser extent in some important personage of every one of the novels of Machado de Assis. Man's egoism is a mainstay not only of the author's best works but indeed of most of his works. Almost invariably, the abject pessimism which colors the outcome of the plots and the fate of the principal characters is a reflection of Assis' conception of nature, environment, and circumstance. The world at large, nature itself, is indifferent to man, and man's egotistic strivings fall victim to an ambient unconcerned with the success of those strivings. Note the author's meaning as he speaks through his protagonist in *Memórias Póstumas de Braz Cubas:* "afeiçoei-me á contemplação da injustiça humana." [8]

Clotilde Wilson, in her explanation of the pessimism of this novel and of *Quincas Borba,* interprets the dark solution which Assis finds for the hopelessness of man's anguished striving in his prison-world as madness, his only refuge. For as he has failed to capture happiness and tranquility in the reality of sanity, he can, in insanity, construct for himself the illusions he desires and achieve thus what he could not achieve otherwise.[9] No one can touch or rob him of the icons he builds in his insanity; they remain his. This, then, is Machado's pessimism, where success

---

[7] Putnam, *Marvelous Journey,* p. 185.
[8] "I resigned myself to the contemplation of human injustice."
[9] Machado de Assis, *Philosopher or Dog?* trans. Clotilde Wilson (New York: Noonday Press, 1954), p. x.

and happiness are to be achieved only in a make-believe reality — that is, in unreality.

So many attempts have been made to arrive at an explanation for Assis' pessimism through the circumstances of the author's own life and social experience that it is difficult to close our eyes to his life in seeking to explain his characters. Waldo Frank, however, has asked this pertinent question: "What will the geneticist ever be able to prove, convincingly, about the relationship of race, disease and poverty to Assis' genius? Precisely nothing." [10] Too heavy a reliance on such an association between author and character is capable of dimming our perspective of the important ideas to be gleaned in Assis' novels.

Let us quickly glance over those novels which have traditionally supplied a basis for the argument of pessimism in Machado de Assis. Braz Cubas has lived a life characterized by wealth, good looks, and health (attributes the author lacked). At various times during his exploits he embraces sex, politics, philosophy, and even "good works." But in the end, as he calculates the sum total of his life, he finds its totality to be negligible, and himself a wretched man. He is consoled that, since he has no children, he will not be cursed with passing on the heritage of a miserable human existence; in this recognition, at least, there is something to be admired.

In *Quincas Borba,* Rubião, Assis' most accomplished incarnation of man's goodness, is unable to purchase happiness either with his material inheritance or with his genuine good deeds: what the indifference of a cruel world has left him is an *illusion* of happiness, only to be reached, even then, in insanity and eventual death.

In *Dom Casmurro,* the innocent, good, and well-meaning Bento becomes transformed into a "Mr. Grumpy," victim of the infidelity of his wife Capitú and the treachery of his closest

[10] Machado de Assis, *Dom Casmurro,* trans. Helen Caldwell with an introduction by Waldo Frank (New York: Noonday Press, 1953), p. 13.

friend, Escobar. Here, however, both evil (Capitú and Escobar) and virtuous folly (Bento) are punished: Capitú dies of ill health, dragged down into prostitution by the current of misdeeds which she earlier initiated; Escobar drowns literally; and Bento is left alive only in body, as he regards, helplessly, the indifferent world which has brought him his despair.

Helena, in *Helena*, after the complicated problems of social convention and family controversy have finally been resolved to permit a felicitous outcome, is so depleted by the strains and anguish her "indifferent ambient" have brought upon her that she dies of a broken heart. So, in *Esaú e Jacó*, does Flora, who cannot decide between Pedro and Paulo. Where Rubião found his escape in insanity, Flora—more symbol than flesh-and-blood human being—finds hers in death, unable to make a decision that will bring happiness to all.

Even Felix, in *Ressurreição*, is cheated of happiness—not by nature or circumstance, however, but by his own inability to believe in the sincerity and goodness of others. His punishment for this is a sterile life without love.

Despite the impressions the above brief summaries leave with us, we still want to ask this question: Is "disenchanted" the final and only adjective to describe Brazil's greatest creator of prose fiction? Or is there perhaps another side of him which has not yet been shown?

We believe that a more careful examination of the author's nine novels reveals a less bleak picture, and that to see that picture one does not need to use rose-colored glasses or to be myopic. One has simply to look for an important theme in the author's work, implicit in *Ressurreição* and *Helena*, and quite explicit in *A Mão e a Luva*. That theme is evident in the characters of *A Mão e a Luva* and in the very outcome of the plot.

Guiomar is the prize. The trilogy of lovers who pursue her is composed of Estêvão—weak, emotional, self-pitying, without will, whose failure in love is presaged by his failure in his professional ambitions; Jorge—superficial, conventional, trivial, and indecisive; and finally, the successful, enterprising, forceful, and well-organized Luis Alves. It is he who, through his ability to bide his time, succeeds in becoming the "perfect glove for the perfect hand." The two ambitious souls are married happily in the end, with the promise of a good life and better things to come. The theme—victory for the strong (those who desire and are able to execute their desires) and failure for the weak (those who are subject to their passions or who have none)—is illustrated in this passage from chapter 17 of the novel: "Will and ambition, when they truly dominate, can struggle with other feelings, but they are sure to win because they are the weapons of the strong, and victory belongs to the strong."

Assis, then, does hold out hope and reward for the fittest, and *A Mão e a Luva* is the classic example of his giving us a choice between failure and success. Whether success is altogether desirable is questionable, but the choice is still there and victory is preferable, at least as far as the participants (if not the author) are concerned. The choice, in fact, is always there, though we do not often encounter situations in which such characters as Luis and Guiomar are present to succeed.

What materialized in Assis' second novel was implied in his first. For even the end of *Ressurreição* is far less than tragic. Felix eventually realizes what the problem is and recognizes the reasons for his shortcomings. He will live on, resigned to his fate, but happy, and we look forward to what the title has promised —his resurrection. He has failed in his projected marriage to Livia, who loved him, but perhaps he will not again.

In *Helena* the choice is also there, for Estacio is neither an undeserving nor weak figure, but his strength and determination alone cannot bring the kind of victory Assis envisages. Helena is weakened and worn; had she endured only a bit longer and more steadfastly, the outcome would have been felicitous.

The equation might have worked just as well for Braz Cubas, Rubião, and Bento. But there is no victory for them because their lack of will power and determination has made them victims of that "indifferent world" over which both Luis Alves and Guiomar triumphed.

Finally, in Assis' last two novels the denouement is far from pessimistic, unless we are looking in the wrong place for their significance. It is true that Flora dies, for she is weak like the others, incapable of coping with the world around her. Yet, the symbol of strength and success in this novel is present in the most important of the secondary figures—Conselheiro Aires, to whom the others carry their problems for solution. Aires also happens to be the protagonist in Assis' last novel.

This same theme of success and happiness for the well-adjusted appears again in the author's last work, which is anything but pessimistic in character. Written in memory of his wife Carolina, *Memorial de Aires* is sympathetic to the loneliness of the aged Aguilar couple. Fortitude, unity of purpose, and strong will are rewarded in the happy marriage of Tristão (successful in politics and his social career) to the beautiful widow Felicia (also of firm character and purpose). Osorio, symbolic of many other unfortunate men like himself, loses his bid for Felicia's hand because of his superficiality and lack of purpose. The tone of the novel, as well as the outcome, is optimistic. It stands with *A Mão e a Luva* as an example of the success possible to those who are strong and enterprising enough to pursue a definite goal, to escape that invisible foe that is Assis' backdrop of despair: the indifferent ambient.

Thus, we may conclude that, in the wisdom which enabled Machado de Assis to portray Everyman's soul in his struggle against the elements about him, he left ajar the door of hope for those endowed with the necessary attributes for passing through it. The only irradicable note of pessimism in Assis, if we look at it thus, is the *difficulty* of seeing the world in brighter terms, not the *impossibility* of doing so.

A number of Assis' works have already been translated into English and have met with considerable success. Among his nine novels the last four are now available. The majority of Assis' works which are on the market in English have been felicitously rendered by Helen Caldwell, who has to her credit Assis' masterpiece *Dom Casmurro* (New York: Noonday Press, 1953), a second edition of which was published in 1966 by the University of California Press, and *Esaú e Jacó* (*Esau and Jacob*), also published by the University of California Press in 1965. At the time of this writing, Miss Caldwell's translation of *Memorial de Aires* is reported to be in progress.

William Grossman has translated *Memórias Póstumas de Braz Cubas* as *Epitaph of a Small Winner* (New York: Noonday Press, 1952), and Clotilde Wilson has given us *Quincas Borba,* published under the title *Philosopher or Dog?* (New York: Noonday Press, 1954).

Finally, Helen Caldwell, with the cooperation of William Grossman, has made available a volume entitled *The Psychiatrist and Other Stories* (Berkeley and Los Angeles: University of California Press, 1963) which includes the *Contos Fluminenses* and the *Histórias da Meia-Noite.*

The first four novels of Machado de Assis are as yet untranslated. It is my hope, with the translation of *A Mão e a Luva* as a beginning, to make available the author's early novels, which remain not only as missing links, but which are meritorious in their own right. For the novels of Machado de Assis constitute a finely wrought chain with nine important links, each of which is a significant milestone on the road to our understanding and appreciation of one of the greatest authors of our time.

The edition of *A Mão e a Luva* used for this translation is volume II of the *Obras Completas,* 31 vols. (Rio de Janeiro: Jackson and Company, 1936). I have updated the spelling of the Portuguese whenever a word was not translated, usually in the case of proper names, and have provided explanatory footnotes wherever it seemed necessary to clarify a work, personage, term, or phrase which might be unclear to the reader.

I wish to express my appreciation and gratitude to my wife,

Nancy Lee Bagby, for her editing of this translation and her constant support of my work. Special recognition is also due my father, Professor Albert Bagby, for his invaluable assistance in the proofreading of the manuscript, and to Professor John Keller for his encouragement in the translation of a work whose importance he never lost sight of. I am also indebted to Professor Helen Caldwell for her prologue to my work. Last but not least, thanks are due my Brazilian friends in Nashville, Tennessee, for their many helpful suggestions.

ALBERT I. BAGBY, JR.

Bibliography

By the Author

1. *Novels or 'Romances'*

   Ressurreição. Rio de Janeiro: Garnier, 1872.
   A Mão e a Luva. Rio de Janeiro: Gomes de Oliveira, 1874.
   Helena. Rio de Janeiro: Garnier, 1876.
   Iaiá Garcia. Rio de Janeiro: G. Viana e Cia., 1878.
   Memórias Póstumas de Braz Cubas. Rio de Janeiro: Tip.
     Nacional, 1881.
   Quincas Borba. Rio de Janeiro: Garnier, 1891.
   Dom Casmurro. Rio de Janeiro: Garnier, 1899.
   Esaú e Jacó. Rio de Janeiro: Garnier, 1904.

2. *Tales or 'Contos'*

   Contos Fluminenses. Rio de Janeiro: Garnier, 1870.
   Histórias da Meia-Noite. Rio de Janeiro: Garnier, 1873.
   Papéis Avulsos. Rio de Janeiro: Lombaerts, 1882.
   Várias Histórias. Rio de Janeiro: Laemmert, 1896.
   Páginas Recolhidas. Rio de Janeiro: Garnier, 1899.
   Relíquias de Casa Velha. Rio de Janeiro: Garnier, 1906.
   Outras Relíquias. Rio de Janeiro, Garnier, 1910.
   Novas Relíquias. Rio de Janeiro: Guanabara, 1922.
   Casa Velha. São Paulo: Martins, 1944.

3. *Theater*

   Queda que as Mulheres Tem Pelos Tolos. Rio de Janeiro:
     Paula Brito, 1861.
   Desencantos. Rio de Janeiro: Paula Brito, 1861.
   Teatro. Rio de Janeiro: Tip. do Diário do Rio de Janeiro,
     1863.

Os Deuses de Casaca. Rio de Janeiro: Instituto Artístico, 1866.

Tu, só Tu, Puro Amor. Rio de Janeiro: Garnier, 1881.

Teatro. Rio de Janeiro: Garnier, 1910.

4. *Poetry*

Crisálidas. Rio de Janeiro: Garnier, 1864.

Falenas. Rio de Janeiro: Garnier, 1870.

Americanas. Rio de Janeiro: Garnier, 1875.

Poesias Completas. Rio de Janeiro: Garnier, 1904.

5. *Criticism*

Crítica. Rio de Janeiro: Garnier, 1910.

6. *Complete Works*

Obras Completas. 31 vols. Rio de Janeiro: Jackson & Co., 1936.

Obra Completa. 3 vols. Rio de Janeiro: Aguilar, 1959.

Obras Escolhidas de Machado de Assis. Ed., Massaud Moisés. 9 vols. São Paulo: Editôra Cultrix, 1960–1965.

About the Author

Alcides, Maya. *Machado de Assis: Algumas Notas Sôbre o Humor.* 2d ed. Rio de Janeiro: Academia Brasileira de Letras, 1942.

Caldwell, Helen. *Dom Casmurro.* New York: Noonday Press, 1953. See introduction.

———. *The Brazilian Othello.* Berkeley and Los Angeles: University of California Press, 1960.

———. *Machado de Assis: The Brazilian Master and His Novels.* Berkeley and Los Angeles: University of California Press, 1970.

Conde, Herminio. *La Tragedia Ocular de Machado de Assis.* Buenos Aires: El Ateneo, 1947.

Grossman, William L. *Epitaph of a Small Winner.* New York: Noonday Press, 1952. See introduction.

Magalhães, R., Jr. *Machado de Assis Desconhecido*. Rio de Janeiro: Civilização Brasileira, 1955.

Matos, Mário. *Machado de Assis: O Homem e a Obra*. São Paulo: Ed. Nacional, 1939.

Putnam, Samuel. *Marvelous Journey: A Survey of Four Centuries of Brazilian Writing*. New York: Alfred A. Knopf, 1948.

Wilson, Clotilde. *Philosopher or Dog?* New York: Noonday Press, 1954. See introduction.

The Hand & the Glove · Machado de Assis

Foreword of 1874

This novel, subject to the requirements of daily publication, came from the author's hands chapter by chapter. Naturally, the narration and style suffered with this method of composition, a bit outside the author's habits. Had he written it under different conditions, he would have given it more extensive development, and a bit more coloring to the characters, which are only outlined here. I ought to say that the drawing of such characters—that of Guiomar, especially—was my principal objective, if not my exclusive one, the action serving only as a canvas upon which I cast the contour of the profiles. Although they are incomplete, I wonder if they might have come out natural and true.

But perhaps I am giving excessively grave proportions to a matter of such little import. What follows is a few pages which the reader will consume in one swallow if they entice his curiosity, or if he has some hour left over which he absolutely cannot employ in anything more beautiful or more useful.

November of 1874.

M. de A.

Foreword of 1907

The thirty and some-odd years that have passed between the first appearance of this novel and its reprinting, now underway, should explain the differences in composition and style of the author. If the author would not have given it the same form now, it is certain he did so earlier; and, after all, all of it serves to define the same person.

It hadn't been on the market for a long time. The author accepted advice in trusting the reprinting to the editor of other books of his. He didn't alter it at all; he only amended typographical mistakes, made orthographic corrections, and eliminated about fifteen lines. Here it is as it appeared in 1874.

M. de A.

1 ' The End of the Letter

"But what do you plan to do now?"

"Die."

"Die? What an idea! Forget it, Estêvão. One doesn't die for so little. . . ."

"One does. If you haven't suffered such pains you cannot possibly evaluate them. The blow was deep and my heart is weak. However grotesque the idea of death may seem, the idea of living is much, much worse. Ah, you cannot imagine what this is like!"

"Yes, I can: a frustrating love affair. . . ."

"Luis!"

"And if in every case of a frustrating love affair a man died, mankind would be greatly reduced, and Malthus' teaching would be wasted. Hurry and come on up."

Estêvão ran his hand through his hair in a gesture of anguish; Luis Alves shook his head and smiled. The two were in the corridor of Luis Alves' house on Constituição Street, which was then called "dos Ciganos" * —then, that is, in 1853, a mere twenty years ago, years which probably have carried away the reader's illusions, leaving in exchange (misers!) a sad, raw, and disconsolate experience.

It was nine o'clock at night. Luis Alves had been on his way home at the exact moment that Estêvão came to look for him; they met at Luis' door. At that very spot, Estêvão confided to him the entire matter (which the reader will learn of straightaway— that is, if he doesn't scoff at these love stories which are as old as Adam and as eternal as heaven itself). The two friends lingered a while in the hallway, one insisting with the other that he climb the stairs, the other insisting that he wanted to die—both of them

* Street of the Gypsies.

so stubborn that there would have been no way to convince either, had a compromise not suggested itself to Luis.

"Why, of course, I agree that you must die, but it shall be tomorrow. Give in and come spend the night with me. During your last few hours on earth, you will teach me a lesson on love, and I shall repay you with one on philosophy."

Saying that, Luis Alves clinched Estêvão's arm, who did not resist this time, either because the idea of death had not cemented itself in his brain, or because he welcomed the painful pleasure of speaking about his loved one, or still, what is more probable, both. Let us accompany the two up the stairs to the sitting room, where Luis went over to kiss his mother's hand.

"Mother, please have tea sent to my room. Estêvão is spending the night with me."

Estêvão muttered a few words to which he attempted lending a humorous tone, but which were nonetheless as funereal as a cypress. Luis saw then, by the light of the candle, a redness in his eyes, and guessed—it was not difficult—that he had cried. Poor boy! he sighed mentally. The two went to Luis' room, a vast area with three beds and chairs of all varieties, two shelves filled with books, and a desk—serving both as study and bedroom. In a few minutes, the tea arrived. Estêvão, after great pleading from his host, took a couple of swallows. He lit a cigarette and began pacing the room from one end to the other, while Luis Alves, preferring a cigar and a sofa, lit the former and stretched out on the latter, crossing his hands upon his stomach blissfully and contemplating the tip of his slippers with that placidity of a man who has known no frustrating love. The silence was not complete; one could hear carriages passing by outside; in the bedroom, however, the only sound was that of Estêvão's boots upon the straw rug.

The two young men were studying at the Academy of São Paulo, Luis Alves in his fourth year and Estêvão in his third. They had met at the Academy and become close friends, as far as was possible for two completely different personalities—or perhaps for that very reason. Estêvão, who was endowed with

6

extreme sensitivity and no less weakness of will, who was affectionate and kind, not the vigorous kindness which is an attribute of strong character, but that soft and waxy kindness which falls prey to all circumstances, had, in addition to all this, the misfortune of wearing upon his nose the rose-colored glasses of his innocent illusions. Luis Alves could see very well with his eyes. He was not a bad youth, but had his share of egotism, and if he was not incapable of affection, he knew how to master it, moderate it, and above all, direct it to his own advantage. Between these two men an intimate relationship developed, born for one from friendship and for the other, from sheer habit. They were each other's natural confidants, with the difference that Luis Alves gave less than he received, and even then, not all he gave expressed great confidence.

Estêvão had been relating to his friend for a long time the entire story of his love, now frustrated—his hopes, discouragements, glories, and finally, the unexpected outcome. The poor boy, paging his way through the most delicious chapter of the romance (in his way of looking at it), had suddenly fallen from the heights of illusion onto the hardest, dullest, and most miserable possible reality.

Estêvão's love—it is time to say something about her—was a girl of about seventeen and at the time, simply a student-teacher at Estêvão's aunt's school on Inválidos Street in Rio. Estêvão had seen her for the first time six months before, and since then had felt imprisoned by her—"unto death," as he had told his friend when he mentioned the meeting, and Luis had laughed at the prolonged period of time. Whatever the fatal length of that captivity, however, the truth is that Estêvão, from the very moment he saw her, loved her, as one loves for the first time—a love a little imprudent and blind, but sincere and pure. Did she love him? Estêvão thought so, and must have believed it—a few soft looks, half a dozen significant handshakes, though at long intervals, seemed to indicate that Guiomar's heart—her name was Guiomar—was not immune to the student's amorous feelings. Outside of this, nothing—or little—more.

7

That "little more" was a flower, not plucked from the garden in its original freshness, but already wilted and without fragrance, and, not given but requested.

"Will you do me a favor?" Estêvão said one day, pointing to the flower she wore in her hair. "That flower is withered and will certainly be thrown away when you take down your hair. I'd like to have it."

Guiomar, smiling, took the flower out of her hair and gave it to him; Estêvão accepted it with the same satisfaction he would have had he been allotted his portion of heaven. Besides the flower and the letters (which did not exist), Estêvão received nothing more during those long six months except the looks mentioned above, which were after all only looks, that disappeared with the eyes they came from. Was it love, a whim, a pastime—or what was it?

On that afternoon, that fateful afternoon when the two were alone together (which was rare and difficult to arrange), he had told her that he was soon to return to São Paulo, and that he was taking a mental picture of her with him, and asked her in return to write to him at least once. Guiomar wrinkled her brow and glared at him with her magnificent brown eyes with so much irritation and dignity, that the boy was astonished and perplexed. One can imagine his anguish during the awful silence which lasted between them for the next few seconds; what one cannot imagine is the pain—the pain and astonishment—which prostrated him when she, rising from her chair to leave, answered him, saying: "Put it out of your mind."

"Well, as for myself," said Luis Alves, hearing for the third time the narration of so bitter a development of affairs, "as for myself, I would obey her to the letter. I'd forget this and go find a cure in my books. Roman law and philosophy—I don't know a better cure for such ailments."

Estêvão wasn't listening to his friend's words; he was sitting on the bed with his elbows on his knees, his head in his hands, seeming to cry. At first he cried silently, but it was not long before Luis Alves saw him lie down upon the bed, twist in convulsions, sob, muffle as best he could the cries which came from within him, pull his hair, ask for death—all this intermingled with Guiomar's name and all of it so completely from the soul, so pathetically natural that Luis finally became moved, and there was nothing to do but to say a few words of comfort to him. The comfort came in time; the pain, having become agony, declined little by little, and the tears ceased, at least for a while.

"I know that all of this will probably seem ridiculous to you," said Estêvão, sitting upon the bed, "but what do you expect? I was living under the conviction that I was loved, and I was, perhaps. For this very reason I cannot understand what happened today. What I supposed was love perhaps only amounted to flirting."

"Perhaps, perhaps," interrupted Luis Alves, cognizant that the best way to cure him of love was to bring to his attention his own self-love.

Estêvão remained pensive for a few minutes.

"No, it's not possible," he retorted. "You don't know her. She is a serious and noble creature, incapable of vulgar or cruel sentiments."

"Women . . ."

"I have already wondered if what happened today might not have been a way of testing me, of seeing to what extent I loved her—don't laugh, Luis, I am not saying anything definite; I am simply saying that it might be. It wouldn't surprise me if she resorted to such a trick; in such a case, a complete expression of her heart. . . ."

Estêvão's imagination raced through this series of florid conjectures, and Luis Alves decided it would be wise not to frighten the horses. His imagination raced, raced, raced along, reins free, and there was a smile on his lips. Have a good trip, exclaimed his friend mentally, stretching out again upon the sofa. It wasn't a long trip, but it produced a wholesome effect on the lover's spirit, sweetening his sorrow—a circumstance which Luis took advantage of, talking to him about a thousand things far removed from the heart in order to divert him from the thought which

9

absorbed him. He accomplished his intention for the space of a half hour, and managed even more, for he caused his friend to laugh, at first a bitter and doubtful laugh, then a jovial and open laugh, incompatible with tragic currents. But, alas! his pain was a sort of moral cough which would abate, then reappear, intensively sometimes, sometimes weaker, but always endlessly. The boy happened to open a page of Werther, read half a dozen lines, and the condition returned, stronger than before.

Luis Alves hastened to his side with the pills of consolation; the condition waned; a renewed conversation, laughter, then despair, and thus the hours of the night drained along, while the clock in the dining room registered them dryly and systematically, as if reminding our two dear friends that man's passions neither accelerate nor moderate the rhythm of time.

Dawn for the two students coincided with the striking of the clock at midday, which is not surprising since they had fallen asleep only after gleams of daylight erased the stars. Estêvão spent the night—morning, rather—tranquilly and without bad dreams. When he opened his eyes, he was confused by the room and his surroundings. He had no sooner recognized them than his heart awakened with his recollection, but without the sharp pain of the day before. The events, though recent, began to mingle with the setting shadows of the past.

Nature has its demanding laws; and man, a complex being, lives not only on love (it must be admitted) but also on food. Let this suffice as an excuse for our student, who ate on that day as on any other; suffice it again to say in his behalf that if he didn't do it tearfully, neither did he do it happily. What is certain is that the tempest had calmed; there remained a hangover, still strong, but it would diminish with the passing of time. Luis Alves avoided talking to him about Guiomar; Estêvão was the first to bring her up again.

"Give yourself time, time," answered Luis Alves, "and you will laugh at your yesterday's plans. Above all, thank destiny for your having escaped in good time. And do you want some advice?"

"Tell me."

10

"Love is a letter, a rather long one, written on vellum, gilt-edged, perfumed and elegant; a letter of good wishes when it is being read, and one of regrets when it is finished. Now that you have arrived at the end, put the epistle in the back of a drawer, and don't think about going back to see if it has a postscript."

Estêvão applauded the metaphor with a good-humored smile.

Twice he saw the beautiful Guiomar before going on to São Paulo. On the first occasion he still felt shaken because the wound had not yet healed completely; at the second meeting, he was able to face her without emotion. It is best—more romantic at least—that I put him on his way to the Academy, the desperation in his heart washed away in tears or drunk up in silence, as manly dignity would demand. But what can I do for him? He left here with his eyes dried, attending to the tedious details of his trip, perhaps thinking of some student prank, a young man again, as before.

2 ⸱ A Robe

After Estêvão had been in São Paulo for a month, his flaming emotion was dead and buried; and he was hailing his recovery with two or three young ladies from the capital, alternately—all of them for diversion. It is certain that two years later, when he received his bachelor's degree, there remained no thoughts of the romance of Inválidos Street. Furthermore, the beautiful Guiomar had long since left the school and gone to live with her godmother. He had not even seen her the first time he returned to Rio. Now he was returning, a graduate in law and social sciences (as has been mentioned previously), more desirous of conquering the future than of reliving the past.

The seat of government was a place of entertainment as it had always been, more or less. Those who had passed the fifty-year mark said that it had been more fun in the past than it was nowadays (the usual charge of those who no longer enjoy the full fruit of their early years). To ripe old men, today's youth never enjoy the fun they enjoyed—a natural thing for them to say since each man sees things through the eyes of his own age. The pleasures of youth are not equally fine nor equally frivolous for every age; but the blame or credit is not to be attributed to youth; it is, rather, the age's that confronts it.

The capital was gay despite the ravages of the recent cholera epidemic; people went on dancing, singing, promenading, and going to the theater. The Casino opened its salons, as did the Club and Congress, all three, *fluminense* * institutions in name and spirit. These were the Homeric times of the lyric theater; the memorable ring of battles and rivalries renewed themselves each season perhaps because of an excess of ardor and enthusiasm, which time either reduces or transfers to matters of less import. Who doesn't recall or hasn't heard tell of the battles waged on that classical stage of Campo da Aclamação † between the Casalonic legion and the Chartonic phalanx, or better yet, between the latter and the Lagruist regiment? These were field battles fought by fresh and seasoned troops—troops prepared with flowers, verses, crowns, and even firecrackers.‡

One night the fight between the Lagruist and Chartonic forces became so violent that it seemed like a page from the

* Typical of Rio, or the state of Rio de Janeiro.

† An area or park in the center of Rio where people gathered in those times to talk and discuss the theater, politics, and whatever else. Its name derived from the Senate's proclaiming Pedro I emperor at that place on October 12, 1822.

‡ At the time in which Machado de Assis wrote, it was fashionable for wealthy landowners to bring over well-known European plays and operas to be presented at a variety of lyric theaters in Rio, most of which centered in the area of the Campo da Aclamação (which no longer bears that name). Distinguished actresses from France, Italy, and particularly Portugal performed in those lyric theaters. It was not uncommon for well-to-do Brazilian young men to court different actresses, and with the competition that developed between these actresses, the opera house became a battleground. Theater-goers split into groups, allying themselves with one or another actress' cause and aired their arguments and defenses in public and private. The terms, then, "Chartonist," "Casalonic," and "Lagruist," refer to the supporters of Madames Charton and Casaloni and Mademoiselle Lagrua, respectively.

12

Iliad. This time, the Venus of the situation emerged from the engagement wounded; a firecracker burst in Charton's face. The furor, the delirium, the confusion were indescribable; the applause and the stamping joined hands—and feet. The fighting moved into the newspapers. "Eternal shame (said one) on the gentlemen who spat in a lady's face!" "If it becomes necessary (retorted another) we will print the names of the critics who, in the foyer of the theater, swore to insult Mlle. Lagrua!"

"Upstart rabble!" "Arrogant frauds!"

Those who escaped those lyrical wars are sure to feel today, after eighteen years, that they expended excessive enthusiasm on something which called for spiritual relaxation and a lesson in good taste.

Estêvão was one of the relics of that Troy, and one of the most fervent Lagruists, before and after getting his degree. The principal reason for his preference was probably the singer's talent, but the reason he usually gave during his hours of leisure (which except for sleeping were the twenty-four hours of the day)—the reason which more than anything else linked him with the "ranks of good taste," he used to say—was (imagine it) the fuzz above Mlle. Lagrua's lip. Perhaps he was not the only admirer of that feature, but I doubt that there was anyone more affected by it than he in this good city. A Machiavellian Chartonist, incidentally a distinguished writer, raised that fuzz to the level of a mustache, suggesting shrewdly that if it was funny, the mustache was worse; and he didn't even want to forgive Lagrua for her lip.

"Oh, that fuzz!" Estêvão would exclaim during the intervals of an opera. "That delectable down will yet be the damnation of many a good man! What wouldn't I give to be perched up there near it so as to get closer to heaven (her eyes, I mean) and to be noticed by her. She is unable to see me in the midst of all her adorers! Do you want to know something? There is where her soul must certainly be, and I should like to amuse myself with her soul, and tell her many a little thing that I feel inside, secrets just waiting for some fuzz that will listen."

Estêvão was more or less the same man he had been two

years earlier. He still smelled of his academic diapers, half student and half doctor, the levity of one and the dignity of the other allying within him as they do in an age of transition. He had the same fantasies and the same simplicity of heart, only he didn't show them in the stanzas he printed in academic journals, which were pervaded with the purest Byronism (a style much in vogue). In them the boy confessed to the city and the world the profound agnosticism of his spirit and his literary ennui. The receiving of his degree interrupted and perhaps ended his poetic calling; the last sighs which sprang from his bosom were some stanzas* to his "lost youth." It is fortunate that he lost it only in verse; in prose and in reality, he was a boy as few were.

The fact that he had done well at the Academy only revealed that he respected more than he actually loved the science of law. His intellectual preferences were divided between, or, more accurately stated, *touched* both politics and literature, and even then, politics only appealed to him with whatever it possessed that was literary. His reading included a little of everything, but all of it was easy and superficial. Estêvão would never understand Lord Macaulay's axiom that it is more profitable to digest one page of a book than to devour a volume. He didn't digest anything; and because of that he had no attachment to the sciences he had studied. He conquered his aversion through self-love; but once the Cape of Torments † had been rounded, he left the matter of sailing on to India up to others.

Naturally, his political aspirations died at the embryonic stage, not only because he lacked the support necessary to strengthen and sustain them, but also because he lacked within himself the strength which is indispensable to every man who aims higher than he was born to achieve.

His aspirations were vague and recurrent, a few legislative and ministerial visions that vanished as quickly as they caught his imagination, or as quickly as he stumbled across the first set of

* *Sextilhas,* a Brazilian poetic form.
† A Portuguese reference to the Cape of Good Hope in Africa, so called because of the many Portuguese ships wrecked there.

pretty eyes, which he did indeed love. He had no opinions; the few writings which he had published during his academic years were a conglomeration of ideas that floated around in his spirit without ever solidifying, coming and going, ascending to one point or descending to another according to his frame of mind at the moment or the latest book he had read.

For the present, he was militating in the ranks of *lagruismo* with the ardor, dedication, and fidelity of a good apostle. He didn't possess the means to afford the luxury of a lyrical opinion; he was born poor and had no relatives in good positions. He had some financial security, which he earned in his profession as a lawyer in partnership with his friend Luis Alves.

One night he had attended the showing of *Othello,* clapping until he tore his gloves, acclaiming until he grew hoarse, concluding the evening satisfied with himself and his own behavior. When the play was over, he went, true to custom, out to watch the ladies leave, a procession of embroideries, silks and fans, veils and diamonds, eyes of all colors and expressions. Estêvão was punctual on these occasions and rarely failed to be the last one to leave. He had his eyes fixed on another pair of eyes, not brown like his, but blue, a royal blue—unfortunately, some married eyes —when he felt someone tap him on the shoulder and utter these words in a very low voice:

"Leave her be; she's not for you."

Estêvão turned around. "Ah, it's you," he said, seeing Luis Alves. "When did you get here?"

"Today," answered his friend. "I am here thirsting for music. Vassouras* has neither a Lagrua nor an *Othello.*"

"You came to cleanse your soul of the dust of the road," said Estêvão, who, though speaking in prose, continued to cultivate his poetic metaphors. "You did well to come; I wouldn't forgive you if you had preferred the other, the insipid one they want to pass off on us here as some great thing and who doesn't even come near the feet of Miss Fuzz. . . ."

* A town toward the interior, between Rio and São Paulo and about 65 miles from the former.

He interrupted himself. Luis Alves had just ceremoniously greeted someone who was passing by; Estêvão turned his head to see who it was. It was a girl, who he wasn't able to see because she was already descending the stairs; but she was so elegant and charming that she excited his admiration.

"Some girfriend?" he asked.

"No, a neighbor."

The procession ended; the two left and went to a hotel to dine, going on later to Botafogo* where Luis Alves had lived since he had lost his mother a few months before.

Luis Alves' house was almost at the end of Botafogo Beach, with another house on its right much larger and more luxurious in appearance. The night was as beautiful as the most beautiful in that area. There was a moon, a clear sky, an infinite number of stars, waves beating languidly on the beach—in short, all the material for a good poetic composition of at least twenty stanzas, rich in rhyme, and a few four-syllable words lifted from the dictionary. Estêvão poetized, but in prose, with a genuine and sincere enthusiasm. Luis Alves, less inclined toward the beautiful, preferred on that particular occasion something more practical— to sleep. He was not able to, however, until he had heard his guest say everything he had to say about those married eyes. "Those blue eyes, as deep as heaven," exclaimed Estêvão.

Finally the two went to sleep; but, either because those eyes persecuted him even in dreams, or because he found the bed strange, or because destiny had so decreed it, the truth is Estêvão slept little, and—as rarely happened—awakened with the first sign of dawn.

The morning was cool and serene; everything was quiet, except for the noise of the sea and the singing of the birds on the neighboring estates.† Estêvão, ill-humored after not having slept, decided to view the morning firsthand. He rose quietly,

* A section or suburb of Rio which is right on the beach.

† The word *chácara* has no exact counterpart in English. This is the best rendering we can give.

16

washed and dressed, and asked that coffee be brought to him in the garden, which he headed for, hugging to him a book that he had found by chance at the foot of his bed.

The garden was behind the house; it was separated from the estate next door by a fence. Scanning the neighbor's garden, Estêvão noticed that it was planted with extreme care and art; many circular rows criss-crossed by two long, straight rows. One of these began at the foot of the stone steps by the house and went all the way to the far end of the grounds; the other went from Luis Alves' fence to the opposite end of the grounds, crossing the first row in the center. From where Estêvão stood, only the second row was visible from one end to the other.

Estêvão seated himself on a bench he found there, took the cup of coffee which the slave brought him soon afterward, lit a cigar, and opened the book. The book was a *Prática Forense*. Let us agree that he was right in closing it and throwing it to the ground with contempt, contenting himself with the singing of the birds and the fragrance of the flowers, and his imagination as well, which was as valuable as both the flowers and the birds. God only knows how far it would have gone with its ready wings if something hadn't roused him and brought him back to earth.

A bathrobe had just come out of the house next door—a bathrobe was all he could see—and it moved along the path that faced the house in a slow and meditative step. Estêvão, who loved all bathrobes, be they meditative or not, thanked providence for the good fortune that smiled upon him, and focused his eyes in order to study the graceful early riser. He still didn't know whether or not she was graceful, but decided she *must* be because he desired her to be.

The delightful vision was finally going to have a soul; the human element was there to crown nature.

Estêvão rose to his full and manly stature in order to see better—and in order to be better seen, let all truth be said—that unknown neighbor who undoubtedly must be the one Luis Alves had greeted at the theater. Actaeon, Christian and modest, did

17

not surprise Diana in her bath, but only as she was leaving it; nevertheless, he shook no less from excitement and curiosity.

The bathrobe went walking along.

3 ⁄ Next to the Fence

The first thing Estêvão was able to discover was that the neighbor was young. Through each opening in the trees, he could see her form, as precise and chaste as an antique piece of sculpture. He could see her milk-colored face, against which her dark-colored hair stood out, not perfectly combed but loosely tied at the top of her head with that early-morning negligence which makes beautiful women even more beautiful. The robe of white muslin, exquisitely embroidered, did not readily reveal the gracefulness of the figure, which seemed and was elegant, of that natural elegance which has been enhanced by culture, demanding little or nothing of a seamstress' touch. She was covered to the neckline, where the robe was fastened together with a small sapphire pin. A button of the same mineral fastened together at each wrist the narrow and smooth sleeves, which were finished with a border of lace.

Estêvão, from the distance and position he was in, could not observe all of the details which I am pointing out to you here, faithful to my duty as story-teller. What he did notice, in addition to the figure, the hair, and the fair complexion, was the girl's stature; she was tall, perhaps a little less than it seemed with the long dress she wore. He could also see a little book opened in her hands, upon which she rested her eyes, looking up from time to time when it was necessary to turn a page, and letting them fall again in order to absorb the words.

She was walking along that way, unaware that anyone was watching her, serene and serious, as though she were crossing a ballroom. Estêvão, who couldn't take his eyes off her, was mentally asking heaven for the fortune of having her closer, and wishing that she would reach the path in front of him. It seemed impossible that she might look prettier to him than she actually was, seen sideways slipping through the trees.

In order not to waste the lessons he had learned earlier, the young graduate was evoking all his literary reminiscences; the young girl was successively compared to a seraphim of Klopstock's, a fairy godmother of Shakespeare's, to everything that was most ethereal, transparent, and ideal in his memory.

While he put his mind to work on these poetic and not, as it happened, ill-suited comparisons in such a place and at the foot of such a charming creature, she had continued along slowly and had arrived at the intersection of the two long paths in the garden. Estêvão hoped that she would turn back to the right, that is, come toward him; he was afraid she might follow along the same path and disappear in the back of the garden. The girl made an in-between choice. She moved to the left, turning her back to her interested admirer, and continued along in that slow, regular step.

The garden wasn't really large, and no matter how slowly the early riser might walk, it wouldn't take her long to get to the end of the path she was walking down. But to that youthful and impatient heart, each minute seemed, well, I won't say a century —that would be to abuse my rights of style—but an hour; it certainly seemed to him like an hour.

The girl, coming to the end of the path, stopped for a few moments and rested one hand on the back of an old bench that faced another at the opposite end. She lowered her other hand and her eyes too, which upset her curious observer. Could it be that she was thinking of someone? Estêvão felt something which I shall call an anticipated jealousy but which was in reality a jealousy of someone else's good fortune. Jealousy is a bad feeling; but in him who was born to love and who in addition had within him the contrast between birth and instinct—that is, an obscure origin and some aspirations to elegant living—in him jealousy was an almost forgivable feeling.

19

The girl turned around and came back down the path. Finally, Estêvão thought to himself, I am going to see her up close. At the same time, fearing that if she saw someone there who was a stranger, she might turn back toward the house, Estêvão moved away from the place where he was standing, with his mind made up to appear when she came near the garden fence. The girl moved along with her book closed and her eyes at times on the ground, at times on the swallows and the wrens that were flitting around the grounds. If she felt lonely, her quiet and pensive face didn't reveal it; indeed, there was not the slightest indication of grief or sadness.

From where he was standing, Estêvão could observe her features without being seen by her; but that is exactly what he did not do from the moment he distinguished them. However, it would have been worthwhile to contemplate those large, brown eyes, half hidden by the long, fine, thick eyelashes, eyes that were neither passionate nor languid, as he had imagined them, but of a sober, chaste, and cold beauty; worthwhile also to notice how they lent to her entire bearing an air of majestic tranquillity and composure. She had not that beauty which, while it subjugates the heart, ignites the senses; her beauty spoke to the intelligence before it addressed the heart. Art as well as nature seemed to have collaborated in that creature, half statue and half woman.

Estêvão was in a position to see and consider all of this. The truth is, however, that he paid no attention to any of these things. As soon as he recognized the girl's features, he remained as though stricken by shock, his eyes wide, his mouth half open, his very life and blood rushing to his heart.

The girl had reached the fence; she stood there a moment, looked around, and then sat down on the bench that was there, with her back to Luis Alves' garden. She opened the book again and continued reading where she had left off, so completely wrapped up in herself and absorbed in the book she had before her that she didn't hear the half-muffled sound of Estêvão's footsteps on the dry leaves. She had covered perhaps half a page when Estêvão, bending over the fence and trying to keep his voice low so that it would reach only her ears, spoke only this name: "Guiomar!"

The girl let out a small cry of surprise and alarm, and turned uneasily to the side from which the voice had come. At the same time, she had risen. The effect which it produced on her (and perchance also an air of irritation that was noticeable in her face) and above all the remorse of not having been able to prevent that cry from her heart caused Estêvão, almost at the same instant, to whisper in a supplicating tone:

"Forgive me; it was a spark from the past that was hidden beneath the coals; it is completely dead now."

Guiomar—we know now that such was her name—gazed seriously and silently at her ill-ventured intruder for two long and mortal minutes. Estêvão, confused and ashamed, had his eyes on the ground; his heart was beating heavily in him as if bidding farewell to life. The situation was too upsetting and embarrassing to be prolonged any further. Estêvão was going to greet her and excuse himself; but the girl, with a smile which was more of pity than of affection, whispered:

"You're forgiven."

She walked to the fence and extended her hand to him, which he shook—I shouldn't say shook, but that he barely touched—as ceremoniously as he could and should have in that situation.

They then stood and looked at each other, daring neither to speak nor to leave, both of them looking at the spectre of the past, that past which for one of them had been so bitter. Guiomar was the first to break the silence, asking Estêvão a perfectly normal question, as normal as could be under those circumstances, but even then, or for that very reason, one of the most cruel that he could hear:

"I believe it has been two years."

"Two years," Estêvão mumbled, trying to hide a sigh.

"You graduated, didn't you? I remember having read your name. . . ."

"Yes, I've graduated. You remember it was my aunt's greatest wish. . . ."

"I haven't seen her in a long time," interrupted Guiomar. "I left the school soon after you returned to São Paulo. I left at the invitation of the baroness, my godmother, who went there to get me one day, insisting that I had nothing more to learn and that teaching was not for me."

"I agree," assented Estêvão. "*My* aunt is the one who didn't leave nor could leave teaching; she ended her days in that work."

"Ended her days?"

"She died."

"Oh!"

"She died about a year ago."

"She was a good soul," continued Guiomar, after a few moments' silence, "very kind and very dedicated. I owe her all I learned—are you admiring this flower?"

Estêvão, caught red-handed in his act of admiration, not of the flower but of the hand it was in—a delightful hand, which must certainly have been the one Venus de Milo lost—spoke shakily:

"It's beautiful, indeed!"

"There are many pretty flowers out here at the estate. The baroness is very fond of these things, and our gardener knows his business well."

The natural timidity of the first encounter disappeared little by little, and the conversation became, while not as informal as in the old days, at least less stiff than it had been in the beginning. There was, nevertheless, a difference between the two: he, despite his unrestraint, felt shaken and upset; she, on the other hand, having got over the shock of the first moment, showed herself composed and casual, always polished and sober, sometimes smiling but with a smile which was on the surface of the face only, and which didn't alter her serenity and composure.

The place and time lent themselves more to idyll than to cold and colorless conversation. A clear and clean sky, pure air, the sun filtering a light through the trees that was yet tepid and

22

wobbly, the surrounding vegetation, all this awakening of things seemed to be demanding an equal dawn in human souls. These souls should have been speaking there their amorous and candid language, instead of another language, courteous, stiff, and formal, which wasn't unpleasant to either of the two, doubtless, but which was much less voluntary on Estêvão's lips.

Guiomar spoke with a certain grace, but a little stiffly and haltingly, with neither vivacity nor warmth.

Estêvão, who had spent most of the time listening to her, observed to himself that the girl's manner was not unnatural, even if in that situation it might have been stilted. The Guiomar which he had known and loved was the embryo of today's Guiomar, a roughdraft of the now perfected panel; she had lacked the coloring then, but the outline of the drawing had been visible.

The conversation lasted about three-quarters of an hour, a mere trifle of time to one who wanted much more. But it was necessary to stop, and she was the first to indicate that.

"You've made me lose a lot of time. We've been here talking for perhaps an hour. It was natural after two years—two years! But what wasn't natural," she continued, changing her tone, "was that I should dare to speak with a stranger in this hardly elegant *déshabillé*."

"On the contrary, extremely elegant."

"You always have a piece of flattery on reserve; I see you didn't waste your time at the Academy. I must go. It's time for the baroness to take her walk around the grounds."

"I wonder if you mean that lady over there at the top of the stairs?" Estêvão asked.

"That's the one," answered Guiomar. "She's waiting for me to come over and offer her my arm."

And with a gesture that was coldly noble, she extended her hand to Estêvão, saying:

"Good day, Doctor, I enjoyed seeing you."

Estêvão touched her fine and soft hand lightly, and bowed respectfully. The girl walked over to the house. He accompanied her with his eyes, admiring the elegance with which, this time at a quickened pace, she slid through the trees and ascended the stairs to the house. He saw her extend her hand to her godmother, and the two walk down the stairs and continue slowly along the path that Guiomar had walked earlier.

Estêvão lingered awhile leaning against the fence, hoping that she would look or walk over in that direction; she nevertheless went by indifferently, as though she were not even aware of his existence. Estêvão left there with his head down and sad, torn by various feelings, full of a sadness and happiness which were difficult to reconcile, and in addition to all this, the vague and deaf echo of this question:

"Am I entering a drama or leaving a comedy?"

4 ′ Latet Anguis

The baroness' walk lasted a little over half an hour. The sun was beginning to get hot, and in spite of the estate's being well shaded, the heat was forcing the good lady to seek shelter. Guiomar offered her arm, and the two, continuing along the same path, returned to the house.

"It seems very late, Guiomar," the baroness said after a few moments.

"It is, *madrinha*.* I took longer than usual today because I ran into someone here at the estate."

"You saw someone?"

"A man."

"Some thief?" the baroness asked, coming to a stop.

"No, ma'am," answered Guiomar, smiling. "It wasn't a thief. My schoolteacher, did you know she died?"

"Who told you that?"

* Godmother.

24

"Her nephew, the fellow I met here today."

"You're not serious! A man here at the house?"

"He wasn't right in our yard, but in Dr. Luis Alves' garden. He was leaning against the fence and we exchanged a few words."

The baroness looked at her for a few moments.

"But child, that isn't proper. What would people say if they had seen you . . . ? I wouldn't say anything because I know you, and I know the discretion God endowed you with. But appearances. . . . What kind of man is this nephew?"

A woman in her mid-forties, tall, thin, and neatly dressed, interrupted them. Sra. Oswald, or as the British would say, *Mrs.* Oswald, had been a companion* of the baroness now for a few years. Mrs. Oswald had met the baroness in 1846; a widow without a family, she accepted the offer the baroness had made her. She was an intelligent and shrewd woman, endowed with a good and helpful nature. Before Guiomar joined her godmother's household, Mrs. Oswald had been the center of attention. The presence of Guiomar, whom the baroness loved devotedly, had altered the situation a bit.

"It's nine o'clock!" the Englishwoman exclaimed from a short distance away. "I thought you must not want to come back into the house at all today. It is extremely warm, Baroness, and you know it isn't wise to expose yourself to this excessive heat, especially during this period of epidemics."

"You're right, Mrs. Oswald, but Guiomar took so long coming after me today that we started our walk late."

"Why didn't you send for me?"

"I thought you would probably be asleep, or busy with your friend Walter Scott. . . ."

"Milton," the Englishwoman interrupted gravely. "This morning was dedicated to Milton. What a great poet he is, Guiomar!"

---

* *Dama de companhia* actually means "lady-in-waiting," a carry-over from old world court usage among the nobility.

"As great as this heat?" Guiomar suggested, smiling. "Let's hurry along, and inside we can hear you more comfortably."

The three hurried along, climbed the steps and entered the vast dining room, whose six windows opened out onto the estate. From there they moved into a little anteroom where the baroness seated herself in her armchair to await the lunch hour. Guiomar left to freshen up; and the baroness, who had had her head down pensively for a few minutes, looked straight at Mrs. Oswald without saying a word.

The baroness was a woman of about fifty, plump, and dressed with a neatness and care which, in old age, was a carry-over from the elegance of youth. Her hair, the color of dull silver, was like a frame around her serene face, a face somewhat wrinkled—not from hard times, for she had had none—but from age. Her eyes sparkled with life, and were the most youthful part of her face.

She had married young, and had the good fortune of being just as happy in old age as she had been in the days of her courtship. Being a widow had cost her much, but several years had passed, and despite the poignant pain which she had experienced, fond memories remained to console her.

"Come closer; I want to speak with you alone," she said to the Englishwoman, who was a few steps away.

Mrs. Oswald went to the door to see if anyone was nearby and returned to sit next to the baroness. The baroness was again pensive, her hands folded in her lap and her eyes on the floor.

The two remained there in silence for some two or three minutes. The baroness finally awakened from her reflections, and turned to the Englishwoman:

"Mrs. Oswald," she said, "it seems to be written that I won't be completely happy. Never has a dream failed me; this one, however, will never be more than a dream, and it was the most beautiful one of my old age."

"But why do you despair?" asked the Englishwoman. "Cheer up, and everything will surely work out. As for my part, I wish I could contribute to this family's complete happiness, to whom I owe so many and such great favors."

26

"Favors!"

"And what else can be said of your tenderness, the protection you have given me, the confidence. . . .'"

"All right, all right," interrupted the baroness affectionately. "Let's talk about something else."

"About her, don't you mean? My heart tells me that with a little patience everything can be worked out. We shall try everything, and everything we try will succeed if it has anything to do with her happiness or yours. 'All's well that ends well' are the words of a poet of ours, a man of great wisdom. In the meantime, I see only one obstacle: a lack of desire. . . .'"

"Only that?"

"What else could there be?"

"Perhaps something else," the baroness said, lowering her voice. "I may be wrong, but I am so unfortunate in my hope that somehow I feel there will be some obstacle."

"But what is it?"

"A man, a young man, I don't know who, a nephew of Guiomar's former teacher. . . . She herself just told me all about it a while ago."

"All about what?"

"I don't really know everything; but in any case, she told me that while she was out taking a walk on the estate, she saw the teacher's nephew next to Dr. Luis Alves' fence and stopped to talk to him. I wonder what all of this is, Mrs. Oswald? Some love which is either continuing or beginning all over again now—now that she is no longer simply the heir to the simple poverty of her parents, but also my daughter, the daughter of my heart?"

The baroness' emotion upon uttering these words was such that Mrs. Oswald took her hands affectionately and tried to comfort her with new words of hope and confidence. She told her further that the simple fact of talking to this man, whom incidentally none of them knew, was no grounds for supposing there had been an earlier love affair.

"Actually," concluded the Englishwoman, "it is difficult for me to believe that she loves anyone in this world. I believe that, for the time being, she doesn't care for anyone, which is to our advantage. Your adopted daughter has a unique personality; she moves easily from enthusiasm to coldness and from confidence to withdrawal. She will certainly fall in love some day, but I don't believe she will experience any great attachments—at least, not long-lasting ones. In any case, I can answer you about the actual state of her heart as if I had the key in my pocket."

The baroness moved disquietedly.

"As for this man," continued Mrs. Oswald, "we will find out who he is, and what amorous relations there were in the past."

"Do you think it's possible?"

"Of course I do."

The Englishwoman spoke with the assurance necessary to calm the good lady's anxiety; the baroness continued to look at her for a while, amazed, as though she were in deep thought.

"There are occasions," the baroness finally said after a few moments of silence, "there are occasions when I almost feel remorse for the love I have for Guiomar. She has come to fill the vacuum in my life left by poor Henriqueta, my own daughter whom death stole from me, to my misfortune. If I had to mourn, it were best to do so with the hope of meeting her in heaven. But I loved her no more than, nor perhaps even as much as this child, whom I have cared for and whose mother God has made me. . . ."

The baroness stopped; she had heard steps in the hallway.

Guiomar, even though she had gone to dress and freshen up, did so in such a simple way that she did not fail to do justice to that "early morning negligence" to which the reader was introduced in the preceding chapter. Her hair style was her own, invented expressly in order to emphasize at once the abundance of her hair and the noble beauty of her forehead. The embroidered edges of a cambric neckline doubled coyly over the blue of the *glacé* dress, fitted and ornamented with an artistic simplicity. This and little more constituted the entire frame of the picture— one of the most beautiful pictures to be found at that time in the entire Botafogo Beach area.

"Hail to my queen of England!" exclaimed Mrs. Oswald when she saw her approach the door of the anteroom.

And Guiomar smiled with such satisfaction and delight upon hearing this familiar greeting that a careful observer would hesitate to say whether this was merely young, womanly egotism, or something more. . . .

The baroness settled her eyes on her adopted daughter, a pair of loving and sad eyes, which the young girl noticed and which made her serious for a few brief seconds. But then she smiled; and, taking her godmother's hands, she placed two kisses on her cheek with such tenderness and sincerity, that the good woman smiled happily.

"You don't have to say anything," Guiomar said, "I already know you think I am pretty. That's what you tell me every day, and at the risk of losing me; because if I become vain, farewell all! No one will be able to cope with me!"

Guiomar said this with so much grace and simplicity that her godmother couldn't help laughing, and her melancholy ended completely. The breakfast bell called them to other pursuits, and us as well, dear reader. While the three are having breakfast, let us glance back to the past, and see who this Guiomar is, so singular and sought after, as Mrs. Oswald put it.

5 ⁄ Childhood

Guiomar had been born in humble circumstances; she was the daughter of a humble public official who worked for some branch of the government, an honest man who died when she was only seven years old, leaving the responsibility of educating and supporting her to his widow. The widow was an energetic woman with a decisive mind; she wiped away her tears with the sleeve of her modest dress, looked at the situation realistically, and decided to fight the battle to victory.

Guiomar's godmother didn't fail her in that difficult period and looked after both of them in the way that she felt it her responsibility. Her concern, however, was not as constant in the beginning as it became later on; other family responsibilities demanded her attention.

Guiomar showed from childhood the attributes which time developed and perfected. She was a gallant and delicate little creature, quite intelligent and full of life, a little naughty, no doubt, but a lot less than is usual in infancy. Her mother, after her husband had died, had no further ambition than to see her married and happy. She herself taught Guiomar to read—poorly, as she herself did—and to sew and embroider, and a little more which she had learned in her role as a woman. Guiomar found no difficulty at all in retaining what her mother taught her, and she tried to learn with such earnestness that the widow, for that at least, felt herself fortunate. "You are to be my little doctor," she often told her, and this simple expression of tenderness would make the girl happy and make her want to work all the harder.

The house they lived in was, of course, modest. There Guiomar spent her childhood—but alone, which is a little more serious. When her mother watched her absorbed in the games appropriate to her age—happy in her childish way, but the kind of happiness that seemed wrong to a mother's eyes—so deeply did their way of life pain her that she often felt the tears fill her eyes. The daughter never saw them because her mother knew how to hide them, but she guessed that they had been there from the sadness that remained in her mother's face. She only failed to guess the motive, but it was enough that if her mother suffered, her own happiness was also diminished.

In time there developed another cause of sadness for the poor widow, even more painful than the first. At the age of only ten, Guiomar developed depressed moods, certain days when she was absorbed in thought and silence—a seriousness which at first was sporadic and rare, but later became frequent and prolonged—moods that were unnatural at childhood, causing her mother to

30

believe that God was calling her back to him. We know that such was not the case. Could it have been the effect of that solitary and austere life which was already molding her personality and, shall we say, helping her to develop strength for the struggles of life?

The first time this disposition became pronounced was one afternoon when she had been playing in the yard at home. The wall in the back had a large opening through which part of the yard of one of the neighborhood houses was visible. The hole had recently appeared and Guiomar had become accustomed to going there to peek through, already serious and pensive. That afternoon, as she was gazing at the mango trees, perhaps coveting the sweet yellow fruit which hung from the branches, she suddenly saw before her, about five or six steps from the spot where she was standing, a group of girls, all of them pretty, trailing their long dresses behind them through the trees and letting their jewels sparkle under the last rays of the setting sun. They went by happily, carefree and contented; one or another might have extended some gesture of courtesy; but they went on, and with them the eyes of the interested little girl, who remained there a long time, enthralled, unaware of herself, still seeing in her mind's eye the scene that had gone by.

Night came; the girl went back inside, pensive and melancholy, without explaining anything to her mother's solicitous curiosity. What could she explain, if she could barely comprehend the impression which these things left upon her? But since all of this made her mother sad, Guiomar conquered her own feelings and became as merry as in the best days.

This was still another side of the girl's personality—she had a willpower far advanced for her years. With it, and with the intellectual vivacity which God had given her, she managed to learn all that her mother had taught her, mastering it even better than her own mother, since time allowed her to develop the first rudiments.

At thirteen she became an orphan; this deep blow to her heart was the first that she was really capable of feeling, and the greatest that ill-fortune had thrust on her. Her godmother had at that time placed her in a school where she was now perfecting what she already knew and learning much more.

At that time the baroness' daughter still lived, an interesting child of about thirteen who was her mother's life and joy.* Guiomar often went over to her godmother's house. The girls' similar ages, the affection which brought them together, the beauty and tenderness of Guiomar, her gracious disposition—all of this strengthened between godmother and godchild the purely spiritual ties that had united them before. Guiomar responded to the sentiments of that second mother; but there was, perhaps, in her affection, although sincere, a certain interest that could seem feigned. The affection was spontaneous; the interest was probably willed.

The girl was sixteen when she transferred to the school directed by Estêvão's aunt, where it seemed to the baroness she could receive a better education. At this time Guiomar revealed a wish to become a teacher.

"There is no other way," she told the baroness, when she confided this aspiration to her.

"Why not?" asked her godmother.

"There just isn't," repeated Guiomar. "I do not doubt nor can I deny the love you have for me; but each one has an obligation he must be true to. Mine is—is to earn my living."

These last words passed through her lips as though forced. Her cheeks became flushed; one might say that her soul covered her face with shame.

"Guiomar!" exclaimed the baroness.

"I ask of you something honorable for me," Guiomar answered with simplicity.

Her godmother smiled and approved with a kiss, an assent with the lips to what the heart could not answer and which destiny would change.

* The phrase "que era tôda a alma e encanto de sua mãe" is ambiguous. The other possible translation, quite different in meaning, is that Henriqueta "was the embodiment of her mother's personality and charm."

32

A short time later the baroness suffered the almost mortal blow to which I referred in the previous chapter. Her daughter died suddenly, and the unexpectedness of the disaster almost carried the mother to her grave.

Guiomar's affection did not fail her in this painful situation. No one appeared to be more affected by Henriqueta's death than she; no one did more than she to console the one who survived her. Her years were but a few; nevertheless, she revealed that she possessed a soul which was at once tender, energetic, affectionate, and resolute. Guiomar was for the space of a few days the real woman of the house; the blow had shaken even Mrs. Oswald.

The poor mother's heart had become so empty, and life seemed to her so dry and deserted without her daughter, that she might well have died of loneliness had it not been for Guiomar's presence. No other creature could have filled Henriqueta's place as she did. Guiomar was already nearly a daughter to the baroness, and circumstances, no less than the heart, had destined them for each other. One day when Guiomar was visiting her godmother, the latter said she would soon come to bring her home to live with her.

"You shall be the daughter I lost; she didn't love me a bit more than you do, nor would I now have any refuge except for you."

"O *madrinha!*" exclaimed Guiomar, kissing her hands.

The baroness was seated; Guiomar knelt at her feet and placed her head in her lap. The dear mother bent over and kissed her tenderly, her eyes fixed upon the daughter which circumstance had given her, her thoughts in heaven where the other daughter must be, whom God had given her and taken back to himself.

Soon after, Guiomar established herself permanently at her godmother's house, to which happiness gradually returned, thanks to the new guest, in whom rare judgment and wisdom were combined. Having witnessed for some time, and not a short while, Henriqueta and her mother's ways of life, Guiomar lent all her efforts to reproducing in the same setting the atmosphere of bygone days so that the baroness would hardly feel the

33

absence of her first daughter. The girl didn't forget any of the other's customs and if she changed anything in any way, it was only to add new ways of serving. Such attention did not escape the baroness' appreciation, and it is superfluous to say that in this way the ties of affection grew even stronger between the two.

As she went along testing and proving her heart's feelings, the girl revealed to no less degree the perfect harmony of her adaptability to the society she had entered. The education which she had of late received accomplished much but not all. Nature had charged itself with completing the job, or, to put it more aptly, with beginning it. No one would guess, in observing the noble, elegant ways of that young lady, that she had come from humble beginnings: on sight of the butterfly, the cocoon was forgotten.

6 ' The Postscript

Luis Alves' advice on that fatal night two years back no doubt was fitting and should have remained on Estêvão's mind. It was not wise to reread the letter, because of the danger of finding a postscript. Estêvão was curious about epistles; it was unthinkable that he not open that one. There was the postscript at the end.

To return to normal language, Estêvão left Luis Alves' garden with his heart half-inclined to love again the woman who had once caused him so much suffering. One might conclude here that he had not really ceased to love her. It is possible; there was perhaps beneath the dying coals a spark—only one spark—that was enough to ignite the fire again. But whatever the case, it is certain that Estêvão left the house with the beginnings of love in his heart.

The entire day was one of commotion and agitation for him, since he didn't resign himself right away, but rather tried to react against the beginning of this new emotion. The attempt was sincere; it was his will that was weak. He tried to dismiss the image of the girl, but it persecuted him tenaciously as though it were a remorse as fatal as the voice of his destiny.

Estêvão said nothing to Luis Alves about the encounter and the conversation which he had had with the girl in the garden, and he didn't hide it out of fear but shame. What could he tell him, though, that Luis Alves had not already seen and perceived? From the window of his room, which faced the garden, he had peeked through the crack in the curtains and had been able to observe them during those three-quarters of an hour of innocent chatting. The spectacle didn't please him very much; Luis Alves thought the choice of locale a bit rash.

The sight of them together attracted his attention because of the coincidence of his neighbor's name and the name of his friend's old sweetheart; undoubtedly, they were the same person.

He's going to tell me everything, thought Luis Alves, when he saw his friend move away from the fence and start toward the house.

Estêvão, as I have pointed out, was discreet. He was preoccupied, far different from the way he had been the day before; and it was easy to read in his face a seriousness which was not customary.

Estêvão had against him both the past and the future. The present offered new hope; he felt that something kept him distant from Guiomar. The past spoke to him of all the sweet memories—the least bitter ones, that is—and his memory almost refused to acknowledge the others. The future was beckoning to him with all its hopes, and it is sufficient to say that they were infinite. In addition to this, the Guiomar which he was now seeing was emerging in the midst of a new setting, one in which he himself preferred to live; but it was appearing, only to vanish again as soon. On top of all this was the obstacle—that closed gate, which could well be the one to the *citta dolente**—but which, in any case, he wanted to open to his ambitions.

The days, woven of gold and black thread, hurried by, alternating between those of confidence and those of disillusionment

* The gate through which the damned pass in Dante's *Inferno*.

35

in a constant battle which ended as it should have and as was to be foreseen. Estêvão followed the impulses of his heart.

To see Guiomar he used every means he could think of. The windows of her house were nearly always deserted. On two or three occasions he happened to see her from a distance. As he approached, the figure disappeared in the shadows of the room. He never missed the theater, but only twice did he have the pleasure of seeing her: once at the Lyrico where "Sonambula" * was being presented; the other, at the Gymnasio where the "Parizienses" † was showing, Estêvão not hearing one note of the opera nor one word of the comedy. All of him, his eyes and his thoughts, were fixed on the box where Guiomar was sitting. At the Lyrico, such contemplation was entirely in vain; the girl didn't even notice he was there. At the Gymnasio, yes, for the theater was small; nevertheless, he would have done better not to have been seen, so obstinately did she swerve her eyes from the place where he was seated.

This didn't keep Estêvão from going to his usual place at the exit to watch for her, placing himself almost in her way, soliciting her eyes and attention audaciously. The family went down the stairs from the second row, next to S. Francisco; the narrowness of the place was excellent. The baroness was escorted by a young, twenty-five year old man of elegant appearance, even if a bit affected. The three of them got to the bottom of the stairs and waited a few minutes for the carriage. In the half-shadows of that place it was easy to distinguish Guiomar's marble face and the refinement of her figure. Her large eyes wandered through the crowd but didn't linger on anyone. She possessed as no other woman the ability to enjoy, without actually seeing it, the homage paid her by the public.

Irritated by the girl's indifference, Estêvão roamed the streets that entire night, alone with his resentment and his love, constructing, then destroying, a thousand plans, each of them more

* An opera by Bellini (1801–1835).
† *Les Parisiens de la Decadence,* a comedy by Theodore Barriere (1823–1877).

36

ridiculous than the other. The cup was completely full; it was necessary to let it spill over upon some friend's bosom, a friend that had in his hands the only remedy he was asking on that occasion—the key to that gateway.

Luis Alves was that man.

"Heartsick again," he exclaimed, laughing when Estêvão told him everything. "I had already perceived it. This business of women. . . . Do you want me to take you over there?"

"I do."

Luis Alves reflected for a minute.

"And what about a trip, wouldn't it do you good to take a trip? I already know what you're going to say, but then, I am not suggesting a trip of leisure to Europe. Listen, if you like, I'll get you a position as a municipal judge. . . ."

The proposition was sincere; Estêvão thought he saw in it a bit of teasing and shrugged his shoulders irritably. The proposition, nevertheless, deserved to be considered; it *was* a career, and it came from a man who was entering political life, who was awaiting the outcome of an election in a few weeks with almost an assurance of victory. It was the birth of influence and it would forcibly grow. But to Estêvão, any public career, law, influence, or future, at this time was summed up in Guiomar's brown eyes.

"I love her," he said, finally, "and this for me is everything. It may well be that you are right; perhaps a big disappointment is in store for me, but these are mere reflections and right now I am not reflecting, right now I am feeling. . . ."

"In any case," Luis Alves offered, "I am carrying out my obligation as a friend; I'm telling you that you two were not meant for each other; that if she didn't love you then, she certainly won't love you now, and that, after all. . . ." Luis Alves stopped short.

"After all, what?" asked Estêvão.

"After all, you're putting me to a test," the lawyer concluded, laughing, "because I have already had a try at her. You don't have to raise your eyebrow; it was a neighborly affair, an adventure that lasted little over twenty-four hours. I say it with embarrassment, for she didn't pay me even a bit of attention and I went back to my papers."

"Well, then, do you like her?" Estêvão asked.

"I think her pretty and nothing else. It was nothing more than a waste of time; if she had accepted I would have married her; she didn't accept. . . ."

"You can see how different we are."

"Then you want me to . . . ?"

"A favor from a friend."

"Very well, then," Luis Alves finally said. "Let your wish be granted. The baroness is going to have some legal business to transact soon and has sent word to me. I am turning the deal over to you; you will enter that house as a lawyer, which in some respects lifts a weight from my conscience."

Estêvão, who only needed a pretext, accepted the offer with open arms, and thanked the giver with such expansive gestures that it made Luis Alves smile.

The promise was fulfilled punctually.

Luis Alves introduced Estêvão to the baroness the very next night as his friend and companion, a lawyer capable of looking after the affairs of such an illustrious client with zeal. The reception was good, generally speaking, except for Guiomar, who seemed upset at seeing him in the house. When Estêvão greeted her like someone who had known her for a long time, she reluctantly returned the greeting; and during the rest of the evening she said nothing further to him. From that source the reception could not have been worse; but Estêvão felt happy as long as he could see her and breathe the same air, asking nothing more for the time being and leaving the rest to fate.

Of all the people in the baroness' household, the first to notice Guiomar's indifference toward Estêvão was Mrs. Oswald. The shrewd Englishwoman sharpened the impassive mask she had brought from the British Isles and never lost sight of the two. Neither the first nor the second time did she see anything other than his eyes, which sought hers, and hers, which seemed deaf. His was, without doubt, a one-sided affair—an unrequited love.

"Did you know I discovered a boyfriend of yours?" she asked Guiomar a few days later.

Guiomar made a gesture of not understanding.

"Please understand me," the Englishwoman added, "I'm not saying you feel the same way about him; I'm simply saying that *he* is in love. Don't you agree?"

"Perhaps."

"I'm referring to Dr. Estêvão."

Guiomar made a gesture of indifference.

"I see that you had guessed," said Mrs. Oswald. "Well, after all, it wasn't hard. One who has a little practice at these things can scent a case of love a hundred miles away, no matter how hard it tries to conceal itself. People in love generally assume that no one is noticing them; it's a pity. I can swear that you aren't in love with anyone."

"What do you know about that?" asked Guiomar, resting her eyes upon her wardrobe mirror. "Well, I am, but with myself."

Mrs. Oswald burst out laughing, a serious and calculated laugh. She knew that the girl was proud of her charms and took the occasion to flatter those feelings. She said many nice things to her, which we needn't go into here, and concluded by placing her hands on her shoulders, looking her straight in the eye, and then breaking into these half-sighed words:

"You're the flower of this land. Who will pluck you? Someone, I know, deserves you. . . ."

Guiomar became serious and gently removed the Englishwoman's hands, murmuring:

"Mrs. Oswald, let's talk about something else."

7 ⸱ A Rival

It wasn't the first time Mrs. Oswald had made reference to something that didn't please Guiomar, nor the first time the latter had answered her with the dryness that the reader observed in the last chapter. The good Englishwoman remained serious and silent some two or three minutes, looking at Guiomar, apparently trying to guess her thoughts, but in reality, not knowing how to get out of the situation. The girl broke the silence:

"All right," she said, smiling. "I see no reason for you to get angry with me."

"I am not angry," retorted Mrs. Oswald immediately. "Why do you think I am angry? I regret, of course, that nature doesn't allow me to have my way and that such a happy union for both is rejected by you; but while this is reason for displeasure, it is not so for anger. . . ."

"Displeasure?"

"For me . . . and naturally for him."

Guiomar answered with a simple shrug of the shoulders which was quick and indifferent, as though she weren't aware of any harm done or at least didn't believe there had been any. Mrs. Oswald couldn't make up her mind which of the two impressions was correct but decided to accept both. The girl, on the other hand, seemed to have regretted her gesture; she took the Englishwoman's hands and, with an even sweeter and softer voice than usual, said to her:

"See what it's like to be a child? Does it seem, on top of everything else, that I am angry with you?"

"It does."

"Well, it's not so. These are the whims of a naughty girl. I made up my mind not to like people to adore me. . . . Wait, I'm lying. I do like that. But what I wish is that people *only* adored me. Don't you see?"

And Guiomar said these words with a cute little laugh and the gestures of a mischievous little girl, which was entirely inconsistent with her habitual seriousness.

"I know, you like a kind of adoration like Dr. Estêvão's, silent and resigned, an adoration that is—"

And Mrs. Oswald, good Protestant that she was, having the Scriptures on the tip of her tongue, continued in this manner, accenting her words:

40

"An adoration such as the kind that Joseph, the son of Jacob, probably inspired, who was as attractive as you. 'Over him the girls would jump fences. . . .' "

"Fences?" asked Guiomar, getting serious.

"The Scriptures say walls, but I say fences because—well, even I don't know why. Don't blush! Mind giving yourself away!"

Guiomar really had blushed; but it was offended pride and dignity which showed in her face. She looked long and coldly at the Englishwoman, with one of those looks which are, so to speak, an indication of an irate soul. What irritated her was not the allusion, which didn't amount to much; it was the inferior and meddling person who made it that she resented. Mrs. Oswald perceived this; she bit the tip of her tongue, but went on with the girl.

"Good heavens!" she said. "It seems you've gotten angry over a harmless joke. You well know that I couldn't possibly want to upset you; to suppose such a thing is to offend me, I who feel a motherly affection toward you. . . ."

The last words calmed Guiomar's anxiety; she had given in to the impulse of her high-strung character. But reason prevailed, and moments later the heart as well, which was not an unkind one. The Englishwoman, who had had much experience in life and knew how to bide her time, made word and action join hands and called Guiomar to her with extended arms. Guiomar went, a little reluctantly, and the conversation would have ended right there if Mrs. Oswald hadn't said to her in the sweetest voice that she could command:

"You might as well learn that I am unreasonable and indiscreet where affection is involved, and this family's happiness is all the ambition my soul has. There can't be any intention better than this. One last piece of counsel—last if you no longer consent that I speak about this. I feel that you perhaps dream too much. Is it possible that you could be dreaming of some romantic love which is almost impossible? I tell you that you are doing wrong, that it is better, much better, to content oneself with reality; if it isn't as fascinating as daydreaming, it possesses at least the advantage of existing."

This time Guiomar had dropped her eyes to the floor with that vague and dead expression of someone who has closed them to external things. Were Mrs. Oswald's words perhaps responding to some silent voice? The Englishwoman followed along in the same pattern of ideas without Guiomar's interrupting her or making any retort. When she finished, Guiomar shuddered as though she were awakening; she lifted her head, and slowly and with emotion, she gave only the following answer:

"Perhaps you are right, Mrs. Oswald, but in any case, dreams are so good!"

Mrs. Oswald shook her head and left. Guiomar followed her with her eyes, smiling, pleased with herself, and murmuring so low that even her own heart could barely follow her fading words: "Not dreams, pure reality."

I suppose the reader is probably curious to know who the fortunate or unfortunate mortal was that the two were talking about in the preceding dialogue—that is, if you hadn't already suspected that he was none other than the baroness's nephew, that young man whom I briefly pointed out to you on the school steps.

He was a young man of about twenty-five or six. His name was Jorge. He wasn't ugly, but artifice had ruined a little the work of nature on him. Too much attention sickens the plant, said the poet, and this maxim is not only applicable to poetry but to man as well. Jorge had a fine brown mustache, groomed and cared for with excessive dedication. His clear and lively eyes would have been more attractive if he hadn't moved them with an affectation which was sometimes feminine. The same can be said of his manners, which would have been easy and natural if they hadn't been so studied and measured. His words came out slow and calculated, as if to make felt all their author's liberality. He didn't say them like most people; each syllable was, so to speak, caressed, making it possible to see after a few minutes that he was making the entire beauty of the expression consist in this elongation of the word. His ideas could be evaluated by his manner of expressing them; they were empty, in reality, but they carried a ring of gravity which made one want to go out and amuse his ear with light and trivial things.

These were Jorge's visible defects. There were others, and of these, the worst was a mortal sin, the seventh. The good name his father had left him and his aunt's influence could have served him well in some good civil profession; but he preferred to vegetate uselessly, living off the wealth he had inherited from his parents, and off the hopes he had of the baroness. He had no other occupation.

Despite the defects in him, he had good qualities; he knew how to be loyal, he was generous and incapable of low deed, and he had a sincere love for his old aunt. As for the baroness, she loved him dearly. Guiomar and he were her principal and almost exclusive affections.

Such was the person whose interests Mrs. Oswald was defending, for love of the baroness and no less for her own sake. The baroness also had her own dreams, as she herself had said, and they were to see those two children happy. Jorge, for his part, was willing to make the sacrifice; considering things carefully, he decided he might well love the girl sincerely. The difference between Estêvão and himself was that his love was as measured as his gestures, and as superficial as his other expressions.

From what has been said, the reader can easily understand that, of the two lovers, only one of them noticed immediately the other's feeling. Estêvão's soul was in his eyes, filling them in such a way that he could see nothing beyond Guiomar.

After two weeks Estêvão's position could be defined as somewhat better; in his own opinion it was excellent. The baroness found out who he was; Guiomar had told her everything. But it was the Englishwoman, no less than Guiomar's words, who made her realize that Guiomar was in no danger; and since the danger was removed, there remained the bachelor's good qualities, which benefited him entirely. Mrs. Oswald's boat traveled the

43

same calm waters. Jorge himself, of course, because he had confidence in himself, didn't fear his rival, and it didn't take him long to loosen up his initial formality. It was not surprising, then, that Guiomar also loosened a little her former rigidity.

Estêvão possessed a wholesome belief in hope, in which, many times, all the blessings of life are summed up. He asked a lot, demanding spirit that he was, but it didn't take much to satisfy him. His imagination was capable of multiplying zeros; with a grain of sand he could build a world. The affability of some and the courtesy of others—these were enough for him to judge himself at the peak of his aspirations; and while Guiomar didn't give him any of the encouragements of bygone days, which were incidentally quite scant, even so he believed piously that love was being born or reborn in that rebellious heart.

Guiomar, in the midst of the loves that surrounded her, knew how to remain above the hopes of some and the suspicions of others. Equally courteous, but equally impassive to all, she looked about her, serenely exempt, neither in love nor inclined toward love. She had at her disposal, if she wanted it, Armida's* art; she knew how to either hold or impel hearts, according to their impatience or coldness; she lacked, however, the desire—or better, she had plenty of that sentiment which she felt was her personal dignity.

8 ⸱ The Blow

One morning Estêvão awoke determined to deliver the decisive blow. Weak hearts have these sudden bursts of energy, and it is a common thing for timid souls to delude themselves. He confessed to himself that he had done nothing and that the situation required that something be done.

* Armida, a character in Tasso's *Jerusalem Liberated*, kept the handsome Renaud imprisoned at her side with her magical charms.

44

Never have circumstances been more appropriate than today, he thought. Guiomar treats me with an affability which is a good sign. Furthermore, there is a noble spirit within her; she will certainly recognize that a discreet and respectful sentiment such as mine is worth a little more than drawing-room flattery.

The resolution was made; there remained the means of carrying it out. Estêvão hesitated a long time between saying in person what he felt and transmitting it by means of the written word. Either approach held for him more dangers than advantages. He feared being cold in a written declaration and incomplete in a spoken confession. Irresolute and hesitant, he adopted, then rejected, both means within short intervals of time; finally, he put off the choice for another occasion.

Chance supplied the solution and the premeditated gave way to the fortuitous.

One afternoon, there being a few people at the baroness' for dinner, the guests went out into the garden for a stroll. Estêvão, who like Luis Alves was one of the guests, moved away gradually from the other groups, and approached that historic fence where, after two years of absence and forgetting, he had seen the now transformed and beautiful Guiomar. It was the first time he had seen that place since the conversation he had had there with her. The turmoil he felt was naturally great; that scene resurged before his eyes—the hour, the shining sky, the sweet smell of the early morning, and finally, the vision of the girl, who appeared there like the soul of the picture, bringing back to him memories he thought dead, hopes he thought impossible.

Estêvão lowered his head at the sweet weight of those memories. His spirit drank up in deep draughts the entire life that his imagination created for him, and perhaps nightfall would have found him in the same mood if Guiomar's soft voice hadn't spoken to him from a few paces away:

"Did you lose something, Doctor?"

He turned his head rapidly and saw the girl as she crossed one of the nearby paths, looking at him and smiling. Estêvão smiled also, and with a presence of mind which is very rare in

45

people in love, especially people like himself, he readily answered:

"No, I have lost nothing, but I have found something."

"Let's see what it is."

And Guiomar, with a firm and sure step came closer, while Estêvão, without hesitating long, forged right there on the spot a philosophic statement about an insect which happened to be walking across a dead leaf. The remark didn't amount to much, and had the effect of coming out a little belabored and improvised; the girl smiled again and was going to continue along her way when he, gathering all his courage, stopped her with these words:

"And what if I had found something else?"

"Something more?" she exclaimed, wheeling around in a light mood.

Estêvão took two steps toward Guiomar, this time determined and resolute. The girl became serious and decided to listen to him.

"What if I had found in this spot, long days of hope and memories, a past which I was sure I would never relive, a hidden and fearful pain, lived in solitude, nourished and consoled by my own tears? What if I had found in this place the torn page of a story that had been started and interrupted, not through anyone's fault on earth, but through the sinister star of my life which an evil angel lit in heaven, and which perhaps no one will ever be able to put out?"

Estêvão became silent and looked straight at Guiomar.

That sudden, face-to-face declaration was so alien to his temperament that she took a few long seconds before recovering from her surprise. He himself was amazed at the boldness he had shown; and while the girl's answer hung from her lips, what had so loosely and confusedly sprung from his bosom at that moment of blessed temerity reverberated in his mind.

"If you had found all of this," answered Guiomar, smiling, "certainly you would have preferred to find something less sad. In any case, it seems you have found nothing more than simply

46

this occasion in which to speak with the lively imagination God gave you. In either case, however, I can certainly pity you or admire you, but it is not given to me to listen to you."

And Guiomar was again about to move away when Estêvão, fearing he would lose the opportunity which fortune had offered him, said from a distance with a sad and pleading voice:

"Listen to me just one minute!"

"Not one, but ten," the girl answered, stopping and turning her face to him, "and they will probably be the last in which we shall speak alone. I give in to the sympathy your state inspires in me; and since you have broken the long and significant silence you've held until now, I will concede to letting you say everything so that you may then hear me speak but one word."

The girl had spoken in a dry and imperative tone, in which the element of impatience dominated more than the commiseration to which she had just alluded. Estêvão's heart was beating in him inordinately, the way hearts beat in those crises of supreme anguish. All those castles in the air laboriously built in his days of illusion—all of them were tumbling and disintegrating like the air they were made of. Estêvão regretted the impulse that had caused him to violate once again the secret of his inmost feelings, to give up so many hopes, nurtured by the best of his youthful temper.

A few seconds went by in which neither spoke; they seemed to be awaiting each other's response, she serene and quiet, he trembling and cold.

"Only one word," repeated Estêvão, "which I am sure will be one to disillusion me. Nevertheless, since I took this chance to tell you part of it, I am forced to tell you all—and to be satisfied if I at least receive the greatest fortune to which I can now aspire— your remorse."

Guiomar had listened to him quietly; the last word made her shudder. Nevertheless, she smiled, one of those somewhat deliberate smiles, and waited.

The narration was long, as long as the occasion, the place, and the person permitted; it lasted only ten minutes. Estêvão hid nothing from her, neither his love for her in the past, nor that which was now being reborn in him, more violent than the first; he told her of the pain he had suffered, the hope which had finally made his soul blossom, everything which he had undertaken in order to have the privilege of seeing her privately, of enjoying at that rare spot on earth the greatest of all good fortune.

This is not a literal but a nonetheless true relation of what Estêvão said during those ten minutes. His words tumbled out nervously and his voice sounded faint, partly because his state of mind had shrunk his throat. His pain was visibly sincere; his eloquence came from the heart.

Guiomar hadn't heard everything with the same expression; at the beginning a smirk seemed to split her lips, but it wasn't long before a more compassionate and humane veil fell over her face. One could see in her an impatience and an anxiety to end the conversation, to escape from it; it was undoubtedly the fear that her absence might be so prolonged as to give rise to suspicion. But there was also commiseration and pity.

"The suffering I have experienced is no fault of yours," said Estêvão, concluding. "Now especially, I—my own mind is the cause of this all. I seemed to see the opposite of what actually existed; I came to believe that you felt something other than total indifference; I see that it was all an illusion."

The tone in which he spoke was just as the words indicate, humble and resigned, without the slightest sign of complaint or reproach. A submission like this had, perforce, to move a woman who was loved. Guiomar spoke to him without acrimony:

"It was an illusion," she said. "But the feeling you have revealed to me no one experiences or nourishes entirely of his own will; nature either promotes or impedes it. Can I be blamed for that?"

"Not at all."

"Neither can you, and I hope this mutual justice will enrich the feeling of friendship we must now have for each other. But there must be friendship only—there can be nothing else—at

48

least from me. Of course, I know that isn't much in a case like this. . . ."

"It isn't little; it's something different," interrupted Estêvão.

"But don't expect anything more," concluded Guiomar without hearing his interruption.

Estêvão opened his mouth to speak but wasn't able to find the words to express what he felt; he moved his hand to his heart, which was beating heavily, and stood looking at her, staring, his eyes vacant, his voice extinct as though his entire soul had vanished. It is certain that after that disappointment there was no reason for him ever to return to that spot, at least not with the assiduousness of hope; and so it was that not even the bitter satisfaction of seeing her was left to him.

"I'll give you one piece of advice," Guiomar added after a few moments' pause. "Be a man, conquer yourself; your great defect is to have retained something of a childish spirit."

"Perhaps," the young man answered, sighing.

"And good-bye. We have spoken longer than it was proper to; I don't know if another would have done this. But I not only recognize your respectful manner but also hope that these few words exchanged now will end impossible aspirations."

Guiomar extended her hand to him, and he touched it lightly.

Meanwhile, the baroness had appeared a short distance away; she was escorted by her nephew who was holding her arm and talking to her, but whom she was no longer hearing. She had fixed her eyes on the two interlocutors of a few moments back. No sooner had the girl observed her godmother in the distance than she quickly gave her arm to Estêvão and the two proceeded along to meet her. Guiomar's face revealed nothing; Estêvão's was perturbed and downcast. The baroness frowned:

"Jorge," she said, "we must have a talk."

9 ⸱ Conspiracy

When the two speakers from the fence approached her, the baroness grew more worried and perplexed. Guiomar was smiling and in a good mood; but Estêvão was disguising his down-trodden state so poorly that one of two things was surely the case: either she had just told him her feelings once and for all, or this was simply a serious mood he was in and one which he either couldn't or didn't want to hide from alien eyes. The baroness thought the latter. However, she concluded that it was of the utmost importance that she attempt something in favor of the former—in favor of the only dream of her old age.

Jorge was not aware of the real reason his aunt had told him she needed to speak to him; he imagined that it would probably have to do with Guiomar and Estêvão, but he was far from perceiving how far-reaching the interview was to be.

It was not possible to have the interview that same day; the guests remained until late that evening and it was the most enjoyable and entertaining evening ever. Guiomar especially had been at her best—charming and vivacious. It seemed as though serenity abided in her soul and mirrored itself in her face, so often pensive but now open and unconcerned.

It is probably not necessary to tell the reader who is discerning and benevolent—(oh! especially benevolent, because one must have good will and a great deal of it in order to have come this far and to be able to continue to the end of a story like this, in which the author is more concerned with painting one or two characters and exposing a few human feelings than he is with doing anything else, because anything else he could not manage to do)—it won't be necessary to tell the reader, as I was saying, that all of that good humor in Guiomar was like a dagger piercing our Estêvão's bosom. He couldn't expect her to be

50

despondent; but at least a little grieved, a little respectful of the pain he felt, yes, this he felt she could be. But she wasn't, and the poor boy left there earlier than he had planned or desired.

In the bedroom, if he could see her later there, alone and all by herself, sitting on the chaise longue beside the bed, with her hair undone, her little feet in her black velvet slippers, her hands in her lap and her eyes wandering from object to object as if they were reproducing on the outside her internal thoughts—in that place not only would he worship her on his knees, but he might even pretend that some preoccupation was keeping her awake, and that this was none other than himself.

Maybe so; at least, in part, it was probably he. Guiomar didn't have a heart so cruel that it could not respond to the sufferings of a man who had seen fit, or unfit, to love her. But be the causes of that worry one or many, the truth is, it lasted a short while only. Guiomar crossed from the armchair to the window, which she opened all the way in order to gaze out at the night—at the moon which reflected the serene and eternal skies upon the waters. Eternal, yes, eternal, my dear reader,* which is the most saddening lesson God could give us in the midst of our agitations, battles, anxieties, insatiable passions, daily pains, and fleeting pleasures, which follow along and end with us underneath that blue eternity, impassive and mute like death.

Could Guiomar be thinking about this? No, she didn't think about this even for a minute; she belonged entirely to life and the world, her heart was just beginning to blossom, she was living in full dawn. What could she care about, or who could manage to make her understand this dry and arid philosophy? She lived for the present and the future, and so great was her future—that is, the ambitions that filled it—so great was it that it was enough to occupy her mind, even if the present didn't offer her anything more. She didn't want to hear about the past; she had probably forgotten it.

Dawn found her sleeping; but the first rays of the sun

* The reference here is to a feminine reader.

wakened her as usual for the morning walk with her godmother. Guiomar was sacrificing everything to her filial dedication which she had already so clearly proved. The baroness, on the other hand, was worried; the walk was different from the usual.

At midday Guiomar got into the carriage with Mrs. Oswald and they went on a visit. The baroness remained alone; Jorge didn't allow her to be alone very long, because he arrived in a short while.

The baroness lost no time with circumlocutions. As soon as she saw her nephew she questioned him formally and directly:

"I have been told—it was Mrs. Oswald who told me—that you like Guiomar."

Jorge wasn't expecting such a question; nevertheless, he was not so naïve that he blushed nor so in love that his voice trembled. He tugged gravely at the cuffs of his shirt, adjusted his tie, and answered innocently:

"I didn't dare talk to you about these things. . . ."

"Why not?" interrupted the baroness. "These are matters that you and I can discuss without its being an impropriety for either of us. Is what Mrs. Oswald told me true, then?"

"Yes."

"Are you really in love or . . . ?"

"I am indeed. I would withdraw if I felt that an alliance between us would look bad for the family prestige; but considering that she is. . . ."

"Guiomar is my daughter," the baroness quickly reminded him.

"Precisely, she couldn't be described better."

"Other things may be said for her," continued the baroness. "She is a celestial and pure soul. Henriqueta didn't have a better heart nor greater love for her own. In addition, nature gave her a superior spirit, so that all fortune did was make amends for the mistake of birth. Last but not least, she is a girl of uncommon beauty."

"*Rare*, dear Aunt, you may say that she is of a rare beauty,"

Jorge added, and for the first time something shone in his eyes that was not like the customary seriousness.

"So you can see," the baroness proceeded, "that she has every right to the love and the hand of a man like you."

The baroness had a naïve and simple heart, not devious nor shrewd; nevertheless, there are occasions in which the most upright person employs, as if by instinct, delicate diplomacy. The good lady had her heart so set on a union between her nephew and goddaughter that she couldn't trust love alone; she was trying to make him interested by virtue of self-love as well.

Jorge bowed with affected modesty.

"A man such as I," he said, "is worth little for his own merit; the merit I have, and I have much, comes from my parents' name and yours, Auntie, and the very saintly qualities which adorn you. . . ."

"One only, Jorge, only one very saintly quality: loving you and her. That's why I was so happy when Mrs. Oswald told me you liked Guiomar. Can you believe that if I were to have the fortune of seeing the two of you united and happy, I would die happy?"

"Oh my! that!" said Jorge, with an air of doubt.

"Do you think such a wedding is impossible?"

"Not impossible; there is nothing that is impossible. But—but I fear that her being in agreement is indispensable, as indispensable as it is doubtful."

"Doubtful! Are you sure of that?"

Jorge had gotten up and taken a few steps, not completely agitated, but a little less impassive than usual. The idea of marriage seemed to him now a little more possible and achievable, since his aunt had openly proposed the alliance.

"Are you sure of that?" repeated the baroness.

"Not sure, but there is every reason for doubt. Guiomar knows that I like her; nevertheless, she gives me not the slightest indication of returning my affection."

Jorge explained in great detail all the reasons he had for

53

believing that Guiomar's wishes did not correspond to his; he told her with the greatest possible exactitude and fidelity three or four episodes which seemed like good proof of what he was saying. The baroness didn't hear everything with equal attention. When he had finished:

"Guiomar is probably very embarrassed," she said, "and sometimes, and for that very reason, she seems cold. There's nothing, though, to keep her from loving you, that is, if she doesn't already. There is in her a certain inherent haughtiness, which can also explain this coldness; it seems to me that she would find it painful to receive love from someone who felt he had to raise her to his level."

"Yes, maybe that's right. . . ."

"But this feeling, which can be and is honorable, is certainly not invincible."

All the baroness' words flattered her nephew, on whose lips there now hovered a smile of intimate satisfaction. From time to time he didn't hear anything of what his aunt was saying to him; his ears turned inward and he listened to himself. Guiomar's love now began to seem possible to him; everything the baroness was saying to him made sense, and had the advantage of clarifying the dark sides of the picture. Besides, up to what point was the baroness guessing or revealing? It could very well be that she might have seen deep into the girl's heart.

Jorge made these reflections while the baroness continued to talk and develop the idea she had just suggested. Until now he had limited his action to a few looks, and some rare words of greeting; the interview with his aunt had given him motivation; it seemed to him the time had come to leave that state of armed peace.

Guiomar arrived shortly afterward and found them in the *saleta de trabalho,* an elegant euphemism which literally means "a room for conversation interspersed with crochet." Mrs. Oswald was with her and both were laughing about some incident which they had seen on the way home. Jorge arose, composed but smiling, and shook Guiomar's hand—really shook it, more than in the usual and courteous way. Guiomar didn't seem to mind; she inquired after his health, extended to her godmother the greetings that were sent her, and started to leave.

During this time, Jorge was looking at her, absorbed in the contemplation of her attractive figure, lovelier now than before, especially since his much-dreamed-of alliance had become possible. There were in Jorge's eyes certain vestiges of sensuousness, from which one might deduce that if he were a poet, and especially an Arcadian poet, he would compose for the millionth time a comparison of the present scene to Venus and her inevitable little loves—a detestable comparison, especially since if the girl's chaste beauty were to be called anything pagan, it should sooner be Diana, converted to the gospel.

Jorge left there singularly agitated; his conversation with the baroness had given him nerve and resolution, and the picture of the wedding began to form in his mind like the watch a boy wears for the first time. Until then he had let himself sail with the breeze; now he could see the necessity and the possibility of reaching the shore of matrimony.

Jorge's doubts didn't prey on his mind; no sooner had he reached home than he took pen in hand and cast upon a white and lustrous sheet of paper an elegant and polished confession, which went through two or three revisions before he decided it was ready. Having completed the final edition, he transcribed the prose from his heart to the neatest piece of paper there was in the house. He folded it and put it in his pocket.

That evening he went to his aunt's house. He found the ladies sitting around a table; for her mother's entertainment Guiomar was reading a French romance recently published in Paris and brought over by the latest ship. Mrs. Oswald was reading also, but to herself, a thick volume of Sir Walter Scott, Constable edition, from Edinburgh.

Jorge came over to interrupt them for a short while, but only briefly, because the reading continued soon afterwards, with him assisting Guiomar in that filial chore. Teatime came and went, as did time to retire, and the baroness closed the session, even though the book was almost finished.

"Only one more chapter," ventured Jorge, the book open in his hands.

The baroness smiled and turned her eyes to Guiomar, to whom she attributed her nephew's sudden resolution; she nevertheless refused, as she was about to fall asleep.

"Well, I'm not going to bed without knowing what happens," declared Guiomar. "I'll take the book with me."

"Ah!" said Jorge with a gesture of satisfaction.

And while Guiomar was preparing to accompany her godmother to the door of the room, and Mrs. Oswald was marking the page and closing her book, Jorge closed his in the same manner, but with such delay and care as to attract the Englishwoman's attention. If she actually understood, we shall find out later; what did happen is that the book was handed to Guiomar with the page marked, not with the ribbon that was there before, but with a little piece of paper.

The little piece of paper was the letter, only a few inches in size; but however small its dimensions, it carried within it no less than a forthcoming storm.

10 ⸱ The Revelation

A half-hour later when Guiomar opened the book to continue her reading, she saw Jorge's letter. It wasn't in an envelope; it was just a small, simple, folded piece of paper which savored of love. Guiomar's mind was so far removed from thoughts of love that she suspected nothing and opened it casually. The first word written was her name; the last was Jorge's.

Guiomar's first gesture was of panic. If he could have seen her through the keyhole and observed the expression on her face, it is very probable that all the love he now nourished would have transformed itself into frustration. But he wasn't there; the girl could faithfully reveal in her face the emotions of her heart.

Another one, she thought. *This one, however. . . .*

And this time the gesture was not of panic, it was of something more, half repugnance, half pity, a strange and improbable mixture.

The girl remained quiet for a while, looking at the paper without wanting to read it, as if hesitating between burning it and returning it unread to its author. But curiosity finally won, Guiomar unfolded the paper and read these lines:

Guiomar! Forgive me if I call you by your first name. Social ethics probably condemn me, but my heart approves. What am I saying? It is the heart that writes these words. It is not my pen, not my lips that speak to you in this way; it is all the living strength of my existence, which proclaims in a loud voice the immense and profound love I have for you.

Before reading of it on this piece of paper you have probably already noticed it, at least guessed it in my eyes, in the sweet intoxication which your eyes produce in mine. I am persuaded that all my efforts in harnessing this affection are in vain; no matter how sincerely I want to forget you, I will never be able to; all I will ever achieve are new afflictions; the remorse of trying to forget you will have surpassed all my other misfortunes.

Why do I today break the silence in which I have kept myself, a fearful and respectful silence which, if it doesn't open the way to glory for me, at least allows me to cling to hope? Not even I could answer you; I speak because an internal force makes me do so, like the river that overflows, like the light that floods the room; I speak because I would perhaps die if I remained silent, in the same way that I shall die of despair, if, in addition to the pardon I ask of you, you do not give me a securer hope than this, which causes me to live and grieve.

Jorge

57

Guiomar read the letter twice, once out of curiosity, the second time for analysis and reflection, and after reading it the second time she felt as cold as she had before she had read it the first time. She looked for a while at the paper, and mentally at the man who had written it; then she put the letter aside, opened her book, and continued the novel.

But her mind, which hadn't remained as indifferent as her heart, began to wander from the novel back to the reality of life with such tenacity that there was no cure but for her eyes to follow along behind it; the girl again sank into the reflections suggested by the case of Jorge's love.

It wasn't passion—at least it wasn't in the full meaning of the word—but something less, or similar to it; and Guiomar saw that it could well be something similar, even sincere. Nevertheless, to what point would her adorer go if she disillusioned him right away; and, given the love that the baroness had for her nephew, to what extent would his being turned down hurt her? Guiomar swept from her mind the fears that were born from such questions; but first she felt them, weighed them before pushing them aside, which should reveal to the reader in what proportion feelings and reason—the inclinations of the soul and the reckonings of life—were combined in her.

Fear having been cast out, the smile returned, that interior smile, which is the most involuntary and cruel one, as well as the least risky, that one can have for human vanity. It couldn't be so despicable as that, the love of a man whose absurdity was compensated for by some good qualities and who was, after all, distinguished, even if his distinction sprang more from an orna-mented and complicated style—which isn't the best. Guiomar saw all of this; but, on the other hand, she couldn't prohibit him from loving her. Still, this didn't make his confession any less fearful.

The girl was also reflecting on the special place which the baroness' nephew had in that house; she couldn't escape being around him, nor probably escape battle, because the pretender would not withdraw under the impact of merely the first blow.

She didn't have this fear with regard to Estêvão; she recognized that his affection was ardent and profound, and therefore more readily inclined toward rashness; but she compared the dispositions of the two men, and if both of them seemed to her of weak moral caliber, she didn't fail to see that the doctor* lacked a certain arrogance which distinguished the baroness' nephew and against which she might have to do battle.

While she made this comparison between the two men, her eyes became a little softer and more languid, a matter of only three minutes, but three minutes which Estêvão would probably have exchanged the rest of his life for, had he known of them. Nevertheless, it was neither love nor longing; a little sympathy, yes, even if only superficial and of little consequence; but above all, it was regret for not being able to love him—or better still—it was a feeling of pity that such a heart was not connected to a different mind.

Guiomar reflected yet a while longer; and she not only reflected, she daydreamed also, giving full vent to the sails of the ship of imagination in which we all navigate at one time or another when we are tired of the firm and solid earth beneath us and when the vast, beachless sea calls us. Her imagination, however, was neither sickly, nor romantic, nor childish; she was thinking neither about going off to gather flowers in some tropical region, nor of falling asleep on the shores of blue lakes. None of this *was* she or *did* she; and no matter how far she sailed, she would carry with her, rooted in her soul, the memories of earth.

She returned at last, and her eyes rested upon the letter; present reality couldn't manifest itself in a worse way. Guiomar arose, irritated, grabbed the paper and crumpled it feverishly; she was perhaps going to tear it when she heard someone knock on the door.

"Who is it?" she asked.

* Assis used the word *bacharel,* meaning gentleman with a university degree, and therefore a scholar (a reference to Estêvão).

"It is I," responded Mrs. Oswald's voice.

The girl went to the door and opened it; the Englishwoman entered, dressed in her nightclothes, with an astonished look which seemed to keep her at a loss for words for a few seconds. Guiomar, afraid, asked:

"What is it? Has something happened to my godmother?"

"May such a fact never come true!" exclaimed the Englishwoman. "Nothing has happened to her; the baroness is sleeping soundly. I came because from my room I thought I heard the noise of footsteps here, and then I saw a light. I thought you might not be feeling well. But from what I can see," continued the Englishwoman, resting her eyes upon the little table where the book was lying opened, "from what I can see, you still haven't finished reading your novel. . . ."

"I haven't read a line since I retired to my room," answered Guiomar, fixing her eyes upon the Englishwoman's face, as if taken by a sudden thought.

"Really!"

"I read something else," the girl continued. "I read this paper."

Mrs. Oswald bent over to read the paper herself, whose contents she had guessed. Guiomar threw it on the table.

"You don't have to read it," she said. "It's a declaration of love."

"From whom?" asked the Englishwoman, opening a pair of astonished and submissive eyes.

"Read the name."

Mrs. Oswald read the signature on the letter, which the girl again presented to her.

"Naturally," continued Guiomar, "this is your doing."

"Mine!" interrupted the lady, a little more sharply than she was usually heard to speak.

Guiomar had gone over and sat down; her impatient little foot was tapping the rug with a rapid and consistent movement; she had folded her arms across her bosom and was looking straight at the Englishwoman with eyes that clearly reflected the

60

irritation she felt. A short period of silence followed; Mrs. Oswald pulled up another chair and sat down close to the girl.

"Why must you treat me unfairly?" she asked, giving her voice a gentle and suppliant tone. "Why aren't you able to see things as they actually are? What there is in this is a curious coincidence, nothing more. If I have talked to you about such a thing a few times, it was because I myself was able to notice the love that Mr. Jorge has for you; it is something everyone can see. I thought that the marriage in this case would please the baroness, to whom I owe so much. Could I have proceeded badly . . . ?"

"Very badly," interrupted Guiomar. "These are family matters which are none of your business."

Guiomar got up, took a few steps, then sat down again. With the movement her hair broke loose and fell freely upon her shoulders. Mrs. Oswald approached to gather it up and tie it, but the girl repulsed her dryly:

"Leave it alone; leave it. . . ."

And she put it back up herself with her small, slim hands, and then gazed at the floor, biting her lip, breathing rapidly, as if trying to control the impetuous and angry word she was about to pronounce. Mrs. Oswald said nothing for a few moments; she waited for Guiomar's irritation to pass. When it seemed to her that the girl had relaxed, she broke the silence.

"I did wrong, I know I did, without a doubt, but my intentions couldn't have been better. Maybe you don't believe me; well, what can I do! What I do ask of you—I won't even ask it; what I piously hope is that you won't attribute to my actions any personal interest. . . ."

Mrs. Oswald paused in order to allow Guiomar to register a protest, but Guiomar didn't protest—I mean she didn't protest openly. She made only a negative gesture, enough to satisfy the Englishwoman's scruples. The girl was sincere; she didn't actually attribute Mrs. Oswald's actions to any evil—mercenary—interests. Neither did she absolve her, not only because she would yet come to cause a painful crisis, but also—it is wise to note it again—because the Englishwoman's position in that house was relatively inferior.

Mrs. Oswald continued to speak in her own defense, justifying in detail the good intentions of her heart, and promising that she would wash her hands completely of that affair, leaving it to her, to the best the girl could do.

"My experience in life," she concluded, "should have taught me that the best of all feelings is a quiet and mute egoism."

While she talked along in that vein, Guiomar seemed to be returning to her habitual tranquillity. The change was not sudden, but a little quicker than it should have been, especially for a person in whom impressions were not superficial nor impulsive. There were even some touches of affability in her face and voice when she began talking, which probably reveals that the change was deliberate and premeditated.

"All right, Mrs. Oswald, let bygones be bygones. I am sorry things have come to this point, and that he would think of writing such a letter, confessing to a love I'm sure is sincere but to which my heart can't respond. You can't order love like you can dresses; above all, it can't and shouldn't ever be pretended."

"Oh, of course!"

"I like him for what he is, my godmother's nephew, and also because she feels a motherly affection for him as she does for me. We're a type of brother and sister, and that's all."

"You're quite right," assented Mrs. Oswald. "You think and speak like a doctor. What can one do? When you don't love, you don't love. He's the one I feel sorry for!"

"He likes me very much, does he?" she asked, fixing her eyes on the Englishwoman.

"Oh! it seems so. You should know that as well as I; I know what I have seen, and I believe that is a great deal."

"I have never noticed anything," Guiomar answered matter-of-factly.

Mrs. Oswald's answer was a smile of incredulity, which Guiomar either didn't see or didn't want to see. There was a pause; Guiomar continued:

62

"But whatever the case, my answer is negative. I am sure that he won't commit against me the injustice of wanting to marry me without my loving him. . . ."

Guiomar stopped, as if expecting Mrs. Oswald to say something to her. This time it was Mrs. Oswald who said nothing, neither with voice nor gesture. The girl bent forward, placed her arms on her knees, her fingers intertwined; and with a smile that was halfway between kindness and affection, she continued:

"You could, in case he ever talked about this to you, or ever does in the future, you could dissuade him from such ideas by simply telling him the truth and giving him advice, the type of advice that you know how to give, and which he will certainly accept because he has a good heart and is a fine young man!"

"Oh, fine! very fine!" responded Mrs. Oswald.

And the two remained looking at each other, Guiomar smiling, but with a smile that was a reflex contraction of the muscles, and the Englishwoman showing an expression of pity, adoration, and regret and a lot of other things which the girl only began to understand when the woman broke the silence in this manner:

"I am wondering whether I should tell you the rest."

"The rest?" Guiomar asked, surprised. "What else is there?"

The Englishwoman brought her chair closer. Guiomar straightened her back and awaited the revelation anxiously, if it was indeed a revelation Mrs. Oswald was going to make. The latter didn't speak right away; it was natural that she hesitate a while and struggle with herself, before saying anything. Finally, in a manner characteristic of one who is gathering all her strength to employ it in something which requires more than her usual courage:

"Guiomar," she said, taking the girl's hands, "no one could ask that you marry without loving your fiancé; that would indeed be an insult! But what I am telling you is that the love which possibly doesn't exist now can come later, and if it did, that would be a great thing. . . ."

"Get to the point," interrupted the girl impatiently.

"It would be a great thing for you, for him, and I dare say for

63

me, who loves and adores you both, but above all, for the baroness."

"How so?" asked Guiomar.

"Oh! for her it would be the greatest thing on earth, because it is her most absorbing and intense wish, truly the desire of her soul. You . . ."

"Are you sure about that?"

"Very sure."

"I don't believe it; I haven't noticed anything that—"

"Believe it; you must. If you promise me you won't say anything about our conversation, nor cause anyone to suspect in any way what I am telling you . . ."

"Speak!"

"Very well, then," continued Mrs. Oswald, lowering her voice as though someone might hear in the solitude of that room and in the deep silence of that house, which was in deepest slumber. "Very well, I'll tell you that I found out about this wish directly from her. When I noticed that Jorge was in love, I spoke of it to your godmother, jokingly, in that intimate way she allows me, and the baroness, instead of smiling as I expected her to, remained pensive and serious for a while, until she finally broke into these words: 'Oh, if Guiomar liked him and they married, I would be completely happy. I have no other ambition on earth. This will be my all-absorbing interest.' "

"My godmother said this?" asked Guiomar.

"Word for word. The answer I gave her was that the marriage wasn't impossible, and that there was nothing more natural than for two people who were indifferent in the beginning to come to love each other. Love many times is born from close contact."

Guiomar wasn't listening anymore to what the English-woman was saying; if she was still looking at her, it was with the vague and vacant look of one who is completely absorbed in private thoughts.

"From that day on," continued Mrs. Oswald, "I felt that I should talk to you on some occasion about this, to sound out your

64

heart, to see if you were in favor of your mother's dream, which would make this entire household happy. . . . I did wrong, I agree, but my intention was the most honorable and upright one in the world."

"Of course," mumbled Guiomar.

Mrs. Oswald took one of her hands and kissed it affectionately. Guiomar didn't repulse her, but neither did she seem to be aware of the Englishwoman's tenderness. The two looked at each other for a few brief seconds without saying anything, as if trying to read the other's thoughts.

Guiomar had neither the experience nor the age of the Englishwoman who could well be her mother; but experience and age, as the reader knows, were compensated for by a great sense of awareness and inherent shrewdness. There are some creatures who reach the age of fifty without ever having gone beyond fifteen, so simple, blind, and innocent does nature make them; to these, nightfall is the prolonging of dawn. Not so with others; they ripen in the spring; they come into the world with the mark of reflection on their personality, though without loss of feeling, which lives in and influences them without dominating them. In these the heart is born harnessed; it trots along, walks, or gallops, like the heart that it is, but it never dashes off; it doesn't get lost, neither does it lose its rider.

What the goddaughter was trying to discover in Mrs. Oswald's face was whether her mother really did nourish that desire, or whether that revelation were merely a trap. The reader knows the truth but will doubtless realize that only after the girl had questioned and examined it thoroughly, would she believe it. She finally did believe it; she believed it because it was true; she believed it because the Englishwoman wouldn't risk any indiscretion on her part which would completely show her for what she was.

"It seems to me," said Mrs. Oswald, "that I didn't do badly in telling you all that I knew. I'm not giving you any advice; the best I could give you isn't worth as much as the voice that speaks from your own heart. Yours is pure and upstanding; inquire into it and you'll find out if there is in it indifference or if some spark. . . ."

"I don't know!" interrupted Guiomar. "I never thought of consulting it."

"You do wrong; it's the timepiece of life. Those who don't consult it naturally remain outside of time. But what do I see!" continued Mrs. Oswald, casting her eyes on Guiomar's little watch. "On that other clock it is ten minutes of one. One o'clock! What would the baroness say if she knew we were still up talking! I'm going; God give you a pleasant rest, and above all make you happy, as you deserve. I won't say be wise, because you have plenty of wisdom. Good night, I'll see you tomorrow."

And Mrs. Oswald tiptoed carefully back to her room.

Guiomar remained alone, sitting at the foot of the bed, listening to the Englishwoman's muffled and careful steps. When the sound died out completely and the silence of the night took over again, deep and sepulchral, the girl let her arms fall on the bed, her face in her hands; and a sigh emerged from her bosom, long, deep, and sad—the first the reader has known since he met her—and finally, these words, wrenched from the soul so painfully—(I was going to say tearfully):

"Oh! my dreams! my dreams!"

She didn't weep; her soul was one of those that has no tears while strength remains. Her eyes were dry and clear when she removed her hands; her face showed signs of distress, but not of discouragement and, even less, of despair.

11 ⁄ Luis Alves

For one entire, long week Estêvão didn't appear at the office where he worked with Luis Alves; he didn't appear in Botafogo either. During all this time no one saw him at the places he regularly frequented. There were six days, I won't say of seclusion, but of complete isolation, because even the few times he went out, he did so only at times and in directions which kept him from seeing or being seen by anyone.

These were the days of that cruel and unfortunate debate, a grave and serious problem indeed, the problem of Ouvidor Street and José Thomaz' house, the ponderous, complicated, exciting question of whether or not Stephanoni would make her debut in *Ernani* * (it is almost certain it would have been a difficult thing to achieve in those days). This matter, which the reader laughs about today as his grandchildren will laugh some day about analogous trivialities, this pretense of Lagrua's, alleging that the *Ernani* was hers, a pretense which made the people and presses of those days groan, was something that was quite adequate to sharpen our Estêvão's wits, as much a general in the smallest matters as a private in the most important ones.

Unhappily, he just wasn't to be seen; he didn't even know about the conflict and the debate, busy as he was fighting the severe and bloody duel of man against himself, when he lacks the support or consolation of other men. He was altogether absorbed in Guiomar; Guiomar was the first and last thought of each day. The girl's shadow lived by him and inside of him, in the book he read, in the lonely street he perhaps strolled, in his nightly dreams, in the stars of heaven, in the few flowers of his neglected garden.

A keen mind, as I take the reader's to be, will make allowances if I don't relate the details of the many plans which he built in his imagination, many and contradictory ones, as is to be expected in such situations. I shall simply mention that he thought on three occasions of dying, twice of leaving the city, four times of drowning his mortal pain in that even more mortal swamp of corruption in which the flower of youth so often rots and dies. In all of this his inner self was only a toy of continuous

* An opera by Giuseppi Verdi (1813–1901).

and varied sensations. The strength and permanence of love were not enough to give sustenance and reality to the undefined thoughts of his brain—sick, even when it was healthy.

The idea of suicide fixed itself further in his mind one afternoon when he had gone out to while away the time and saw a funeral procession going by on its way to Cajú.* The cortege was pitiful, even more so because of the indifference that was written on the faces of those accompanying the casket. Estêvão came to his senses, and sincerely wished he were inside, stuck between those narrow pine boards, with all his pains, passions, and hopes.

I have no other way out, he thought. *I must die. There is only one pain and then there is freedom.*

As he returned home, the sight of a child playing in the street, wading in the muddy water of the gutter, caused him to stop for a few seconds and envy the good fortune of childhood, which laughs with its feet in a dirty puddle. But envy of death and of innocence were replaced by envy of happiness when, as he was nearing home, he saw through the open windows of a neighboring house the lighted sitting room and a bride-to-be crowned with orange blossoms, smiling at her fiancé, who was in turn smiling at her, both with that indefinable and unique smile typical of that special moment.

The five days went by in this fashion, filled with irritation, despair, tears, bitter thoughts, and useless sighs, until the morning of the sixth day shone, and with it, or a little after it, a letter from Botafogo. When Estêvão saw the baroness' servant at the front door with a letter in his hand, he became so excited he didn't hear a word the messenger said. Could he have thought the letter was from Guiomar? Possibly. But the illusion lasted the few seconds it took him to tear the envelope and unfold the piece of paper that was in it.

The letter was from the baroness.

* A suburb or quarter of Rio located in the Zona norte, or north section of the city.

68

The baroness asked graciously if he had died, and requested that he come over to discuss her business. Estêvão had got to the state where he was only waiting for an excuse to break his vows to himself; there couldn't be a better one. He rapidly wrote two lines in answer, and at one o'clock in the afternoon he was stepping down from a carriage at the door of that calamitous and delightful house where he had spent the best and worst hours of his life.

"Do you know why I have imposed on you this way, in addition to the pleasure of wanting to see you?" the baroness asked as soon as the first greetings had been exchanged.

"You said it had something to do with that 'request.' . . ."

"Yes, we have to get a few things straightened out before we leave."

"Madame is leaving the capital?"

"We're going to the country."

Estêvão became pale. In his situation, such a trip was the best thing that could possibly happen to him; nevertheless, the news had a bad effect on him. The conversation that followed was all about the business of law, and it lasted a long hour without Guiomar's having appeared at all. On leaving, Estêvão dared to ask about her.

"She's out riding somewhere," answered the baroness.

Estêvão said good-bye to his client, who accompanied him all the way to the door of the living room, reminding him of a few points which the lawyer barely heard and certainly didn't remember.

The hope of seeing the girl, more than anything else, had caused him to go to that house; now he was leaving without the pleasure of having seen her even once—worse than that—in danger of not seeing her soon if ever again. He was beginning to reflect on this as he approached the door, where at that same moment a carriage was stopping. Estêvão naturally trembled, even before seeing who was about to get out of the coach; he stayed close to the gate with his eyes fixed upon the carriage door, while a little slave was hurrying to open it.

69

The first person who got out was our friend Mrs. Oswald, who did so without giving Estêvão time to offer her his hand. As soon as he saw her, he rushed up to the carriage door.

Guiomar got off immediately behind her. Her hand, in her tightly fitted, pearl-colored glove rested lightly on Estêvão's hand, which trembled all over. The girl smiled a greeting and went on into the house with the Englishwoman. It wasn't much, but little as it was, it excited the young lawyer, and from there he went straight to town, to the office.

Luis Alves was surprised to see him; it wasn't a six-day surprised look as it should have been, but a forty-eight-hour one at most. Nothing unusual about that, however. Luis Alves' preoccupation those days was his candidacy in the election; the good news should arrive by the first mail from the north. Understandably, a man who is about to be enrolled in the ranks of Parliament doesn't have time to be thinking about the love plaints of another, even if the young man involved is his friend and the love a genuine one.

Estêvão lost no time with soliloquies; at once distressed and consoled, he entered spilling out his soul on his friend's shoulder. After each portion of full confession that he made to Luis Alves there, he received in answer a comment, sometimes serious, sometimes humorous. Nevertheless, when Estêvão gave him the news about the baroness' family going to the country, the half-smile which had been on Luis Alves' lips from the beginning disappeared, and with sudden and sincere astonishment, he exclaimed:

"To the country?"

"The baroness told me just now."

"But . . ."

Luis Alves didn't finish; he looked at Estêvão still half doubting, then remained silent for a while, scratching his chin with his ivory letter opener and looking at the picture that hung on the wall in front of him.

"Considering the situation I'm in," Estêvão continued, "you are sure to say that the trip is a blessing in disguise. Well, it's

70

not; I can't agree to such a trip; if she leaves the city, so will I."

"You're crazy!"

"Maybe!"

Luis Alves now left that natural indifference he had customarily used in hearing and talking about this subject. He spoke kindly to Estêvão, perhaps for the first time in his life. What he said to him was nothing more than an expanded version of what he had said before, this time with greater meaning, because of his formal reproof at the hands of Guiomar. There remained no other recourse except to forget her altogether.

"Oh! that, never!" interrupted Estêvão. "Furthermore, I don't know. I'm not sure that she was speaking from her heart that afternoon. . . ."

The candor with which Estêvão said this was a true revelation of his attitude, and don't seek a reason for such words, reader, unless you consider that smile of a few moments ago, there next to the carriage, a smile that was prancing in his mind like rays of sunshine filtered through black and stormy clouds.

Luis Alves shook his head and focused his eyes on some sheets of scratch paper and political documents in front of him, which he started to finger through slowly. Suddenly he delivered a light blow to the papers with the palm of his hand, and lifted his head:

"There is a way to find out everything," he said, "to find out if she really loves you, or . . . I'll be glad to try it for you on one condition."

"What's that?"

"On the condition that you withdraw any designs you have on her. What the devil do you gain in nursing a love that has no hope of success or a happy outcome?"

That was the hardest promise that could be wrenched from a heart in which generations of hope succeeded one another almost without end. Nevertheless Estêvão made it, perhaps with the secret intention of breaking it.

A few minutes later Luis Alves was alone. The last words he spoke to his friend were a couple of boyish pleasantries, but as

71

soon as he was alone he became serious and, leaning forward and placing his arms on his desk and cleaning his fingernails with his pocketknife, he remained there a long time as if reflecting, his thoughts far from Estêvão, who incidentally was no longer anywhere nearby, and even farther away from the documents he had in front of him. But what could he have been thinking about, if it wasn't Estêvão, nor the documents, nor for the moment even his election hopes? Be patient, reader, as you will find out in time. May it suffice to say that after an absence of twenty minutes, Luis Alves returned to his senses, enunciating in a loud voice only this:

"There's no doubt about it; she's an ambitious girl."

And released from that worry, he buried himself completely in the subject matter of those documents.

12 ⁄ The Trip

Luis Alves had hardly returned to the reading of his tracts when his servant came in and handed him a calling card.

"Have him come in," said the lawyer, reading the name of the baroness' nephew.

And immediately the slow and measured step of the young man could be heard in the hallway; in no time he was at the office door, extending a formal but gracious greeting.

"Have I come at the wrong time, Doctor?" Jorge asked.

"For heaven's sake," exclaimed the lawyer, rising and going to the door to meet him. "There's never any wrong time for you, and especially now. I am so tired of reading these papers that the greatest thing I could hope for is the presence of a man of wit."

Jorge thanked him for the compliment, which had been a little too emphatic, and answered with an even more extensive and far-reaching piece of flattery, which meant that he had come to ask for something. After the first few moments of formal

72

introductions and frayed generalities, Jorge stood up straighter than he had already, but said abruptly:

"You know, I'm here to ask something important of you."

Luis Alves bent forward.

"Important and at the same time not difficult," the baroness' nephew continued. "But before I do I must know whether or not you're as much a friend of our family as we are of yours?"

"Oh! certainly!"

"You're perhaps one of the persons who come over least, even though you're a next-door neighbor, although I *have* seen you come more often recently. In any case, you're like a flower betrayed by its perfume. My aunt has a very fine opinion of you; she feels you are very serious, and I feel the same thing— although, mind you, I don't really understand how a man could be any other way. These restless souls. . . ."

"They're unbearable," concluded Luis Alves, anxious to get to the point of the visit.

The point was the baroness' trip. About two years earlier the widow had promised a *comendador,** a friend of the late baron's and a rancher at Cantagalo,† that she would spend some time out there. The baroness had always avoided fulfilling her promise; now, however, the insistence had been so great that she had decided to go. What Jorge had come to propose was a *conspiracy* —his word—of friends to dissuade his aunt from that project. He assured the lawyer that even if the conspiracy was discovered, his reputation wouldn't be endangered.

Luis Alves thought at first that this was only a pretext; but having observed that the beautiful Guiomar was not indifferent to the young man's advances, he realized that the former had an entirely personal interest in the proposed conspiracy. After all, Jorge actually confessed that if his aunt insisted on leaving the city he had no recourse but to go along also.

It was not difficult to reach agreement; they decided to make

* An honorary title, usually military, given to a person of distinction; comparable to "Knight."

† A town in the interior.

every effort to dissuade the baroness from going. Jorge wanted to leave right away; Luis Alves kept him a while longer with expressions of praise ably introduced and even more ably woven into the conversation. He also let himself follow along in the other's frame of mind, accepting his ideas and preconceived notions and applauding them discreetly, serious when they were so, or seemed to be, laughing when they were humorous—responding, that is, to the other's every gesture and maneuver as does a mirror, because it is obliged to and has no choice—in summary, employing the whole art of diplomacy, of attracting and intriguing men, an art which he had learned early and which would profit him later on in public life.

That same night Luis Alves went to the baroness' house where a few close friends of the family had gathered. The mistress of the house, sitting in her customary chair, had next to her a woman of about her same age, also a widow, and in front of her the white and retired sideburns of a former civil servant. Over on a sofa were Mrs. Oswald and Jorge, talking in a sometimes low and other times louder tone. Farther down, two young men were relating to two elderly women the plot of the latest play at the Gymnasio. Farther away, one neighborhood girl was bragging to another about Mme. Bragaldi, whose skill with the scissors was as accomplished as that of her husband, the set designer, with the paintbrush.

Finally, near one of the windows was a lively and pretty young lady uttering a thousand trivialities to another person, who was none other than our acquaintance Guiomar. Thus divided, the conversation sometimes became general, only to fall back immediately into its previous particular topics; the groups also changed around from time to time, as did the subject matter, and in this fashion the hours, poor things, which could neither defy nor slow their pace even one minute, moved on enjoyably.

Luis Alves had joined the baroness' group, and Jorge did not delay adding himself to it. The lawyer had the discretion to allow the subject to come up in its own time, if it came, or to maneuver it into the conversation when it seemed propitious. But Jorge,

74

who was impatient, forced the subject into focus. Luis Alves proved himself true to his promise. He declared lovingly that as a friend and neighbor he was against the trip, and that if necessary he would call on public support, for it was an error and a crime to leave that house destitute of the goodness and graciousness and taste and all the other excellent qualities which the fortunate people who frequented it could always count on finding there. Finally, to leave was so ill advised that it couldn't be considered anything but a sin that, while not pointed up in the catechisms as a sin, would certainly have to be punished with bitter consequences in the centuries to come, so that, with further amendments, it was his decision that the baroness should stay.

All of these points were expressed and made as they should have been, in a gallant and debonair manner which the baroness answered in like fashion. And the conversation wouldn't have gone on if Luis Alves, changing his style, hadn't given the subject a different turn.

"Let's be honest, Madame Baroness; the trip is sure to be immensely uncomfortable for you, if nothing else; your strength, certainly, is not the same as it was in your earlier years; your health is unstable and can't stand such a taxing journey. I confess that I speak in the name of the personal interest I have as a friend and neighbor; but the main reason is not that. If there were an urgent reason for you to leave, well, that would be different; but since it has to do only with a promise made such a long time ago, it would be cruel on my part not to insist that you stay."

The baroness was trying to defend her position, but it didn't take Luis Alves very long to realize that she wasn't speaking with the vigor of a resolution that originated with her. The conversation, in the meantime, was becoming rather general and from all sides there began to emerge opposition to the trip.

Several minutes had gone by in which Guiomar had not been listening to the girl she was speaking to; her ear was tuned to her mother's group. No one noticed her; but it is the privilege of the writer and the reader to see in the face of a character that which

75

others do not or cannot see. We can read in Guiomar's face not only the weariness which that unanimous opinion against the baroness' project caused but also the expression of an imperious and willful mind.

"I believe we are in agreement, then?" asked Luis Alves, looking alternately at the baroness and at the other people.

"It's just not possible, Doctor," the good woman answered.

"Of course it's not possible," intervened Guiomar from the place where she was sitting. "The trip offers no risk nor is my godmother an invalid. Furthermore, a promise has been made; it can't be broken."

This opinion, expressed in a flat and firm tone, even if the voice didn't lose any of its natural softness, was the equivalent of a little cold water thrown upon the triumphant boiling of emotions.

"Guiomar is right," said the baroness. "I can't change my mind now; it is only for three or four months."

Luis Alves gazed long at Guiomar, as if trying to see in her face all the foregoing reasons given to substantiate the baroness' resolution. The opposition weakened; Jorge called the lawyer to his aid in vain. His aunt's resolution, if it had at any time been shaken, was again firm.

Guiomar, in this interim, had gotten up and walked over to join her mother's group. Jorge looked at her with an expression of egotism and jealousy. Luis Alves, who was standing, moved back a little in order to let her by. The eyes with which he looked at her were neither egotistical nor jealous. The female reader, who probably remembers the confession he had made to Estêvão, will possibly suppose they were of love. Maybe. Who knows? A love a little restrained, not crazy and blind like Estêvão's, not trivial and lascivious like Jorge's, but midway between one and the other, such as would be the case with an ambitious heart.

"Dr. Luis Alves defends cases," said Guiomar, smiling at him. "It's not a matter of its being impossible. As for myself, Cantagalo has only one inconvenience; it won't be as much fun as the capital; but time goes by rapidly. . . ."

76

"In that case," said Jorge, sighing, "I can also dispense with theaters and balls; I give in to the family's wishes."

"You want to go with us?" the baroness asked happily.

"Undoubtedly!"

Guiomar bit her lower lip with an expression of displeasure, which she was able to control and mask without anyone's noticing, anyone, that is, except Luis Alves. A tranquil and shrewd smile lightly touched the lawyer's lips, while the girl, in order to hide the expression that remained on her face, returned to the window where she had been and remained there for a few moments alone, half bending out of the window and half hidden by the shade of the curtains. A sound of steps made her turn back inside. It was Luis Alves.

"Ah!" she said, pretending to be calm. "Let me thank you for not having insisted further with your advice."

"My intention was good," answered Luis Alves in a low voice. "But now it will be excellent. All is not lost; leave it to me to save the rest."

Guiomar frowned, with a true look of surprise; with such a look that it seemed to have made her forget another feeling, equally natural: that of the displeasure which that singular familiarity should have caused her. But the surprise of the moment dominated everything. Guiomar felt that he had seen in her the reason for the insistence and her displeasure with the result.

The scowl disappeared gradually, but the girl didn't move her eyes away for a while. There was in them an imperious question, which her soul dared not transmit to her lips. If there is any question in the reader's eyes, let's await the next chapter.

13 ⸱ Explanations

Luis Alves had grasped the entire significance of the expression in Guiomar's eyes; nevertheless, he was a cold and resolute man.

He bowed with grace and gentility, and said to her as politely as was possible for one so strong and austere:

"You feel I was a little daring, don't you? I was merely sincere; and even if your refinement condemns me, I am sure your heart forgives. . . ."

Guiomar had pulled herself together.

"You are mistaken," she said. "I don't condemn you, for the simple reason that I didn't understand you."

"All the better," replied Luis Alves without batting an eye. "In that case, I erred only within the sphere of my intention."

"But . . . were you referring to the trip?"

"Yes, I was; I was asking when you were leaving."

Luis Alves' presence of mind set very well with Guiomar's personality; it was a point of communication. The girl answered that the *comendador* was coming to get them in fifteen or twenty days.

"Only three months?" asked the lawyer.

"Three or four."

"Four months isn't an eternity, but Cantagalo for a true *carioca** is sure to be a place of exile, or nearly so. I hope," continued Luis Alves, concluding more rapidly than he wanted to on seeing Jorge approach the window, "I hope this exile won't let you forget what I'm solemnly going to tell you now: you have a great and refined personality, and I admire it!"

Jorge was there; the conversation either had to end or take another direction.

Luis Alves' last words were singularly calculated to leave a deep impression in the girl's memory. His remark was neither a declaration of love nor a ballroom courtesy which she had heard many times and which could and did flatter her; it was more than a courtesy and yet it was not quite a declaration. There was no emotion in the lawyer's voice; there was firmness and an air of deep conviction. Guiomar gazed at him almost without becoming aware of Jorge's presence; but Luis Alves had turned to

* Native of Rio.

78

Jorge and was already speaking to him in a light tone—quite different from the one he had just been using.

If this contrast was deliberate—I don't know whether it was —it couldn't have been better suited to the mind of Guiomar. Of all the men she had previously dealt with, he was the first that inspired curiosity in her, and also, on that occasion, the first person who was feeling sorry for her. Will the reader please take notice: *curiosity* and *gratitude*. Are there any two more appropriate wings to hurl one soul into the bosom of another, or into an abyss, which is sometimes the same thing?

I said "feeling sorry," and these words alone, without being accompanied by any other or anything else, might cause the reader to think that during those days when we lost sight of Guiomar, she had become an unfortunate creature. Not so; the situation was the same, not the same as before Jorge's letter, but the same as it was on the night she received it, a situation doubtless quite somber and threatening for a heart that is afraid of being embarrassed, but which is neither desperate nor in anguish.

If the baroness had known the facts, or if she could have deciphered them in the girl's manner, she would have been the first to extend to her every possible consolation. But she didn't know. Her wish—or rather, the dream of her old age, as she put it in one of the previous chapters—was that she pass on, leaving her nephew and goddaughter happy, and she felt that the best way to see them happy was to bring about their marriage. The information she had about the girl's affections in this respect was incomplete or inaccurate; what was repugnance was interpreted as coldness. Mrs. Oswald was constantly giving her hopes of happy and impending success; the girl's anxieties she never mentioned. The baroness hadn't found out about Jorge's letter nor about the incident in the bedroom. The marriage continued to appear to her to have all the probabilities of a realizable hope.

The female reader will probably feel that the baroness' nephew didn't deserve so much concern and persistent hope in his behalf and she is probably right; but the baroness' eyes are

79

not those of the reader's. All she could see was his good side, which he really possessed, even if it was only of a relative goodness; but she was unable to see the bad side; she couldn't see the frivolous gravity of his personality, nor the kind of love that was growing in his heart.

Jorge was her only blood relative, son of a sister that had lived unhappily and died even more unhappily, not repudiated, but disliked by her husband—a circumstance which made that young man dear to her. More than her goddaughter, no; not that, nor as much, certainly; her heart wasn't big enough to be divided equally in such large portions; nevertheless, she loved him very much, enough to want to see him happy and to work toward that end. Let us add that her sister's fate was always in her mind, and that she feared a similar fate for Guiomar; she felt that she could see in Jorge all the necessary attributes to make her happy.

Unfortunately, Mrs. Oswald, who well knew those secret desires and who was, more or less, a confidante of Jorge's feelings, felt that this was a perfect time to show all the gratitude she possessed and the deep friendship which bound her to the baroness' family. She wove herself in to please others, and herself even more so. She appreciated the difficulties but didn't lose hope; it was necessary to make the baroness' wishes known. For this reason she didn't hesitate to let Guiomar know her godmother's wish, exaggerating it in the process, because the baroness had never said that "such a wedding was her one concern"; Mrs. Oswald had only attributed to her the phrase, deadly as far as the girl's hopes and dreams were concerned. But if she spoke too much to one, she was much more careful with words before the other, and from her exaggeration or attenuation of the truth had resulted that never-ending state of hidden battle, of fears, indecisions, and secret bitternesses. It is wise to say, in order to give the picture a final stroke of the brush, that Mrs. Oswald wasn't listening only to the voice of her own personal interests, but also to the impulse of her very personality, dedicated to testing its own shrewdness, to undertaking and accomplishing one of those delicate and difficult operations in such a way that if there were

80

such a thing as domestic diplomacy, or if positions were being created for her, Mrs. Oswald could count on a job as ambassadress.

Returning now to the narration of the story, I should tell the reader that Jorge's letter received neither a written nor a verbal answer. On the day following its delivery he went out to Botafogo for dinner, but Guiomar remained in her room on the pretext of having a headache; the baroness spent the day with her; all Jorge was able to find out when he left there was that she was better. In the days that followed, no answer reached the suitor's hands, neither did he manage to have five minutes alone with the girl. With that supreme art a woman possesses of scheming and tantalizing, which goes hand in hand with her being in love, Guiomar always managed to slip away.

One day, however, there was no way to get away, and Jorge, who had no feeling in his voice because he had little in his heart, looked at her directly and asked frankly for either a word of hope or a word of discouragement. The girl hesitated for a few seconds, but it was necessary to answer. She overcame her repugnance and said to him with a cold smile:

"Neither one nor the other."

"Not even a sign of discouragement?" Jorge asked, ruffled.

"One can't give either," she said. "We just usually accept what destiny bestows."

That wasn't really answering, as the reader can see for himself; Jorge was going to ask for a more tangible decision, but the girl had taken advantage of the lull and had slipped away. When he recovered his voice, all he could see was the hem of her dress disappearing around a door.

Guiomar shortened the reins of the familiarity that existed between Jorge and herself; however, if she treated him with more reserve, she didn't do so with dryness nor coldness, nor did she fail to be polished and friendly. The natural dignity she possessed served her as an ivory tower, where she could ensconce herself and keep her suitor respectful.

Of the two men who loved her, neither spoke to her soul;

Estêvão, she felt, belonged to the phalanx of the "lukewarms," Jorge to the tribe of the incapables, two types of men that had nothing in common with her chosen affinity. Of course, she didn't place both suitors on the same level; one was only sentimental while the other was trivial; but neither was capable of creating, of his own will, his destiny. If she didn't equate them, neither did she see them with the same eyes. Jorge was monotonous; he was a new type of Diogenes; through the tawdry cloak of his superciliousness his sad vulgarity throbbed visibly. Estêvão inspired in her a little more respect; his was an ardent but impotent soul, born to desire and not to win, a kind of condor, capable of looking at the sun, but without wings to fly to it. Guiomar's feelings with relation to Estêvão could never develop into love; there was too much superiority and pity involved.

If she had been of a different personality and had different aspirations and lived in another setting, she could probably have loved him as he loved her. But nature and society had joined hands to lead her away from those purely intimate pleasures. She wanted love, but didn't want to enjoy it in an obscure life; the greatest happiness on earth would become to her the greatest misfortune if she were left in a desolate region. As a child, her eyes had followed the silks and jewels of the women she saw on the grounds opposite her mother's modest yard; as a young lady her eyes followed the brilliant spectacle of social grandeur. She wanted a man who, in addition to having a youthful heart that was capable of loving, felt within himself the necessary strength to place her upon a pedestal where she could be seen by all. Only once had she voluntarily accepted obscurity and mediocrity and that was when she was planning to follow the teaching profession; but it must be said that, in that, she had been able to count on the baroness' loving tenderness.

14 · Ex·Abrupto

The reader has already become aware that the trip to Cantagalo was almost exclusively Guiomar's doing. The baroness had fought it at first, as she had on other occasions, and the *comendador* no longer had much hope of seeing her on his farm. But Guiomar's vote was decisive. She strengthened the *comendador*'s arguments with her own, alleging not only the obligation her godmother had of keeping her word, but in addition, the advantages that those three months of country life would have for her, far from the agitation of the city. Summing it up, she pointed to her own desire to see a farm and to become acquainted with the ways of the interior.

There existed no such desire nor anything similar to it; but Guiomar knew that on the scales of her godmother's resolutions, the fulfillment of a desire of hers was of great weight. The sacrifice would last three or four months; she would face, however, ten or twelve, if such were necessary to escape Jorge's intentions for a while, even though she found repugnant any kind of living except the splendid and agitated life of the capital. I, who am the Plutarch of this illustrious lady, will not fail to point out that in her endeavor there was something of Alcibiades, that foppish and delightful statesman who, because of contempt, also was able to bear Spartan frugality.

Unfortunately, Jorge reduced all these calculations to nothing. She was counting on his excessive attachment to the pleasures of the court; she was not counting on Mrs. Oswald's suggestions, who had noticed the plan and twisted Jorge's first resolution, which was to remain and hope. The sacrifice on his part was compensated for by the probability of victory, which consisted not only in having for a wife a beautiful and sweet girl but also in making much larger the hereditary portion which the baroness would leave both of them when she died. This consideration, which wasn't the principal one, did, even so, have weight in Jorge's mind. And let us be fair, it should have; to possess was his only profession. So it was that not only would the girl be failing to receive one reward, she was also falling from one evil into another, even greater; to have him close to her, where diversions would be fewer and less varied, was the same as becoming ill from boredom and dying of inertia.

For this reason, one can imagine Guiomar's state of mind after Jorge's declaration. There was no way to escape the suitor; it was necessary to endure him. Such a prospect totally weakened her vitality. A confidante in such situations is a gift from heaven; Guiomar had no one, and if anyone had merited such confidence from her, it is certain or almost certain that she wouldn't have told her anything. Her afflictions sprang from pride; the sadness of her heart, from modesty. Persons of this kind ignore the consolation that is to be had in moments of crisis by sharing with others, a sad but happy type of ignorance which many times spares them from contact with a perfidious and evil soul.

In the midst of her long soliloquies, the words of Luis Alves reverberated in her memory; she heard them again, exactly as he had said them, from the discourteous phrase to the respectful expression. One was the corollary of the other, and both could make clear to her Luis Alves' character, if there were still elements in it to be known; in any case, the tip of the veil had been lifted. Even though the depths of his mind couldn't be read, one could see in this his method of action.

Any other man, after the effect produced by the first declaration, either wouldn't dare or wouldn't consider it important to try anything else to spoil the plans for the trip. But Luis Alves was as obstinate as a bulldog. It was important to him that the baroness' family not leave the capital; this he was going to accomplish no matter how he did it. He watched his opportunities, took advantage of circumstances, and managed to insert the request in every bit of conversation where it would have seemed least appropriate to anyone else. Jorge applauded him with all the strength and force his interests could muster. The baroness opposed the lawyer's suggestion with the weak and clumsy resistance of one who desires the very thing she is refusing.

"The doctor is terrible," she would say. "When he gets something in his head, no one can get it out."

"Precisely; it is an *idée fixe*. Without a definite idea nothing good can be done in this world."

Guiomar supported her godmother's decision, though she didn't do it often nor in the same dry and imperious tone as the first night. Her impulse was to be consistent; at the same time she didn't want it to appear to Luis Alves that she was accepting his help to obtain what she supposedly wanted with all her heart; this would be to absolve him of his first fault.

The argument which most influenced everyone's thinking, the one which eventually did away with the idea of such a trip, was the danger of facing the cholera which at the time was hitting some of the places in the interior. One morning it became known that this terrible scourge had appeared at Cantagalo. This time Luis Alves triumphed without saying a word; the baroness capitulated before that brutal fact.

The trip was given up, therefore, to everyone's satisfaction, except perhaps Mrs. Oswald's, who greatly feared the young men of Rio and Guiomar's beautiful brown eyes. Mrs. Oswald feared that with each step there would appear a new enemy, ready to ambush at some theater or ball, or if not, on Ouvidor Street, and she couldn't see that the new enemy was literally knocking at the door. The Englishwoman's shrewdness this time was somewhat blind. The reason was that Luis Alves, in all his maneuverings, had conducted himself ably; far from seeking the girl out, he seemed not to have altered his feelings, nor did he seem to want to change the type of relationship which he had until then maintained. Guiomar, on the other hand, couldn't help but compare that type of attentive indifference which he had toward her with the words she had previously heard him speak; and the result of the comparison wasn't very clear to her.

On the night of the same day in which it was decided to

postpone the trip until a better occasion, there were a few out-of-town people at the baroness'; Guiomar, seated at the piano, had just finished playing, at her godmother's request, a portion of an opera that was in vogue.

"Thank you very much," she said to Luis Alves, who had approached in order to compliment her. "You're happy! It must be the satisfaction of having spoiled the greatest wish I had for the moment."

"It wasn't I," he said, "it was the epidemic."

"Your ally, it seems."

"Everything is an ally to the man who knows how to desire," answered the lawyer, giving to this somewhat emphatic phrase the greatest tone of simplicity he could utter.

Guiomar lowered her head and for a few moments continued running her fingers over the keys, while Luis Alves, picking up another piece of music from the piano, said to her:

"You could give us this piece by Bellini, if you wanted to."

Guiomar took the music mechanically and opened it up on the rack.

"Was it your wish, then?" she asked, continuing the subject of the interrupted dialogue.

"It certainly was, because it was necessary."

"Necessary!" she retorted, beginning to play, less for playing's sake than to cover the sound of her voice. "But why necessary?"

"For a very simple reason: because I love you."

The music stopped. Guiomar jumped up. But neither the girl's move nor the surprise of the other people disturbed the lawyer; Luis Alves leaned over toward the piano bench as if straightening it and turning to Guiomar, he said to her graciously:

"You may sit down now; it's fixed."

Guiomar sat down again, mute, annoyed, her heart beating in a way it had never beat at any time in her life, not from fear nor pique nor . . . love, I was going to say, without ever having been in love. She didn't stay there long; her hand trembling, she fingered through the pages of the music that was opened on the rack; then she quit and got up.

No one noticed these last movements; if anyone had, the girl's actions would have dispelled all suspicions. The first impression was profound, but Guiomar had enough strength to control herself and to lock her feelings up in her heart.

What happened later when free from public eyes, she was able to give in to her feelings, no one knew, except the silent walls of her room, or the ray of moonlight filtering through the fine material of the window curtains, which spied on that soul hungering for light. Perhaps her mirror found out the following morning as it reflected her disfigured face and tired eyes. Whether it was the nocturnal meditation which had softened her eyes and dulled them, the mirror didn't ask, because it knew, but perhaps it occurred to the mirror that if they looked more beautiful that way, they needed another face in which they would fit better. The face wanted them as they were, severe, resolute, and brilliant.

The baroness also didn't fail to notice that her goddaughter hadn't awakened with the same air as usual; she found her uncommunicative and absentminded.

"I, *madrinha*?" asked Guiomar, feigning a smile of surprise. "My eyes are probably fooling me."

"It must be that; I am the same as I was yesterday, and shall be tomorrow. I had a rather bad night, it's true, but whatever it was I had, disappeared entirely. The proof of that . . ."

Guiomar stopped at that point, approached her godmother and gave her a kiss.

"The proof is that you still find me pretty today, don't you?"

"Child!" answered the baroness, giving her a loving tap on the cheek.

The girl's tranquillity was forced; as soon as her godmother had turned her back, the shadow again covered her face. She had learned in childhood to hide her feelings.

As for Luis Alves, while he had counted on his crude and abrupt method, he left there without positive certainty of the results. This uncertainty shook him more than he knew; and it was, without a doubt, the first time in his life he felt that he really loved, even if his love was just like *he* was, placid and sure of itself. On the following day Estêvão questioned him about Guiomar.

"I believe," he said, after reflecting for a few moments, "I believe that for the moment you shouldn't lose all hope."

15 ⸱ The Trouble with Go⸱Betweens

For three days Luis Alves kept himself from going to the baroness' house, and was, as a matter of fact, about to die over it. This absence, however, entered into his plan; it was one of the instructions which he himself had given his heart; there was no way but to observe them.

On the fourth day he received a note from the baroness congratulating him on being elected. The mail from the north had arrived and with it the news of the election victory. Luis Alves was a representative; he was finally going to have a hand in the making of the laws. Estêvão was the first to congratulate him; he was his old "companion of the bench" at the Academy; it was his place, as much if not more than others, to applaud his friend's good fortune. He didn't, however, hide from him the jealousy he felt.

"A representative!" he sighed. "Oh! if I could also be a representative."

Estêvão said this like the child who wants the trinket he sees around the other child's neck—nothing more. It was yesterday's dream, being reborn just as it had once been, inconsistent, vague, ready to disappear with the first morning ray.

Luis Alves hurried over to the baroness' to thank her for her congratulations. Guiomar trembled slightly when she saw him, but received him composed and smiling, almost indifferently. The lawyer was clever; he didn't follow her with his eyes; besides drawing other people's attention, it would be to follow the usual pattern. He didn't want to look like all the others.

Guiomar, on the other hand, looked at him off and on for periods of time, as if wanting to catch him unawares; little by little, however, her gaze became more direct and straight. Luis Alves' gaze continued natural, the way it was before, and the way it was now with everyone.

Near the front door, where he ran into her by chance on leaving, Luis Alves had the opportunity to ask her this simple question:

"Have you forgiven me?"

The girl pulled her hand away, which he had caught tightly in his, and pulled back, lowering her eyes.

"Have you forgiven me?" he repeated.

Guiomar withdrew without saying a word. Luis Alves waited for her to disappear from sight, then he left. Meanwhile, the girl became irritated with herself for not having answered him, although it is true that she neither had nor probably would have had anything to answer. But she was sorry she had done it and thought about it a long time.

Does that mean that she loved him? It means she was beginning to. The dawn whitened the sky; it would later tint the top of the hills, and finally spill itself down the slope, until the sun appeared—the sun, contemporary of Adam and of the last man to come into the world.

A few days later, as Luis Alves entered the baroness' house, he had the good fortune of finding the girl alone in the "work room," which the baroness had left about five minutes before. Mrs. Oswald was out. It was late afternoon; the day was about to fade into the darkness of night.

Guiomar, relaxing in a low chair, had a book open over her knees, her eyes in the air. Luis Alves caught her in that pensive attitude, more beautiful than ever, because that way and at that time and with her semidark dress emphasizing her creamy-white face, she had a certain comely but serious something to her which seemed made to order for receiving him.

"My godmother will be right back," said Guiomar after extending her hand to him, which he shook and found a little tremulous.

"Perhaps in about five minutes," he said. "Enough to decide my destiny. Twice I asked you if you had forgiven me; for the third time I am asking you to answer me; it doesn't take much; only one word; it would take even less, only a gesture."

The girl looked at the book she had in front of her. But the morning of her heart was already high, the daylight was intense and the sun hot and alive, because she didn't look at the book very long nor did she hesitate more than was natural and appropriate under the circumstances. Two minutes later she made the gesture, only one gesture, but even more eloquent than if she had spoken—she held out her hand to him.

Luis Alves held it tightly between his own. The tumult was natural in both of them; there they remained for several moments, quiet, he with his eyes fixed on her, she with hers on the floor. Their hands touched and their hearts beat in unison. Five brief minutes went by that way. She was the first to break the silence.

"One gesture, only one gesture, and it is my entire destiny I give you with it," said Guiomar, looking straight at the young man.

"Not yet. If our destinies unite, I am convinced that my love, at least, will have the virtue of making you happy. But nothing is decided yet, and if I was brief and hasty in my confession, I don't want to be in the dedication I ask of you."

Luis Alves stopped; the girl looked at him as though trying to understand him.

"That's right," he continued. "It's best you don't give in to a moment of enthusiasm. My life is yours; my entire destiny is in your hands; nevertheless, I don't want to surprise your heart at this moment; on the day you find me truly worthy of being your husband, I'll listen to you and follow you."

The girl's answer was to squeeze his hands, smile, and drink up his eyes in hers. The baroness' footsteps interrupted the interview.

Guiomar was really in love. But to what point was that feeling spontaneous? To the point of not causing the purity in our heroine's heart to fade, to the point of not diminishing the strength of her conscious faculties. Only up to that point; from there on the free choice of her mind entered in. I don't want to portray her as a person whom love disrupts and blinds, nor as one who might die of a silent and timid love. None of these was she, nor would she be. Her nature demanded and loved those flowers of the heart, but that wasn't to say that she would go and pick them in wild and barren places, nor from the branches of a modest bush planted in front of a rustic window. She wanted them beautiful and luxuriant, in a Sèvres vase, on top of a rare piece of furniture, between two urban windows, the vase and flowers flanked by cashmere curtains, dragging their tips on the carpeted floor.

Could Luis Alves give her this type of love? He could; she felt that he could; their two ambitions had divined each other's from the moment intimacy brought them together. Luis Alves' procedure, sober, direct, resolute, without idle or weak spells, enabled the girl to see that he had been born to win, and that his ambition really had wings, while at the same time his heart also had them, or seemed to have them. Furthermore, he had taken his first step toward becoming a public figure; he was going to enter squarely on the road which carries the strong to victory. He was going to be surrounded by light, which was the girl's ambition, the atmosphere she wanted to breathe. Estêvão would give her a sentimental life; Jorge a vegetating life; in Luis Alves she could envision domestic warmth combined with the bustle of noise outside.

Once they understand each other, it is difficult for two hearts to hide, at least from the shrewdest eyes. Mrs. Oswald's were of the shrewdest. Before long the Englishwoman perceived that there was something between them. To question the girl was useless in addition to being dangerous; it would probably be like deliberately asking to be hated. But what if it were still possible to save everything? It would be very hard for Guiomar to resist a wish of her godmother's; on this point, she might defeat the girl.

Mrs. Oswald then conceived of a rash project, which to her seemed excellent and wise. Her desire to please the baroness and to finish what had been started blinded the truth from her eyes. She went straight to Jorge.

"Do you know what I think?" she said. "I think there are Moors on the coast."

"Moors on the coast!" exclaimed Jorge with such an expression of displeasure that it was easy to see there was probably already some suspicion in the back of his mind.

"Nothing less," said the Englishwoman. "But a Moor that can be captured."

And the Englishwoman outlined a complete plan to which the baroness' nephew listened, somewhat perplexed. The plan consisted in Jorge's going to the baroness and asking for the girl's hand in her very presence. The baroness, who nourished the desire to see them married, would not fail to cast her vote, and it would be very unusual if Guiomar's gratitude didn't decide her in favor of Jorge.

"Gratitude and *interest*," she continued. "We must also count on interest, which is an intimate counselor. She certainly won't want to take a chance on losing her godmother's affection, which to her is worth . . ."

"Oh! what an awful thought!" interrupted Jorge, recoiling before Mrs. Oswald's idea.

The Englishwoman smiled and didn't insist on that argument; she held on, however, to the one about affection. Guiomar would not oppose a wish of her mother's; it was urgent to deliver the blow against her. Jorge didn't want to gain the girl's acquiescence in that manner; but he did believe in its being effective, and above all he feared losing his cause. Once it had been won, he could leave the rest to time and to his own love.

The advice was promptly followed. That evening, in the

92

presence of the baroness and at the time to say good-night (because he had hesitated all night), Jorge performed that ill-advised act, declaring to the girl that he loved her and asking her for her hand. His aunt smiled with contentment but was wise enough to say nothing, while Guiomar, becoming pale, said nothing because there was nothing to say.

The silence lasted about three or four minutes, an embarrassing and vexed silence in which no one had the nerve to resume the conversation. As for the baroness, she assumed the two had had an understanding and that the proposal was sanctioned by the girl. Guiomar's air of confusion was not of the kind that would make such an assumption logical; but the good woman saw only with the eyes of her good wishes.

"For my part," declared the baroness finally, "I'm not opposed; I would be very happy to see you united. But it's a matter of the heart; I must await Guiomar's answer."

And turning to her goddaughter:

"Think and decide, my child," she said, "and if you are happy, I will be also, even more than you."

Twice the negative reply almost fell from the girl's lips; but her tongue dared not repeat the decision of her heart. After a few moments:

"I'll think about it," she answered, kissing her godmother's hand; and then, turning to Jorge:

"Good night! I'll see you tomorrow!"

16 ⁄ The Confession

On the same night that Jorge, yielding to Mrs. Oswald's suggestions, was attempting the last recourse which from her point of view existed, Luis Alves was at home seated comfortably in a leather armchair in front of the window, his eyes on the sea and his thoughts on his two recently won elections. The clock was striking midnight; someone got out of a carriage and was knocking at his door.

It was Estêvão.

Naturally, Luis Alves was surprised to see him there at that hour, but Estêvão explained everything to him.

"I've come to spend a half hour with you, or all night, if you wish. I was at home, upset, thinking . . . you know about what. . . ."

"About her?" interrupted Luis Alves.

"Now and always."

Luis Alves twisted his mustache and watched his friend while Estêvão took off his hat and was preparing to draw up a chair to sit next to him.

"Estêvão," Luis Alves said, after a few moments of reflection and as he turned his chair around, "listen to me first and you can decide whether or not you'll spend the night or leave immediately. Perhaps you'll choose the latter."

"Are you going to talk to me about Guiomar?"

"Exactly."

Estêvão seated himself in front of Luis Alves. His heart was beating rapidly; one might say that his whole life was hanging from his friend's lips. There was a moment of silence.

"No hope . . . no hope at all, then?" Estêvão whispered.

"You said the fatal word!" exclaimed Luis Alves. "Yes, there is no hope for you."

"But . . . how do you know?"

"Don't question me; I cannot tell you all there is to tell. Spare me that sad duty, at least."

Estêvão felt his eyes fill with tears. He tried to speak but his words came out enveloped in sobs.

Luis Alves was smoking tranquilly, following with his eyes the little circles of smoke that escaped from the end of his cigar. This silence lasted about ten minutes. The sea was beating rhythmically on the beach. The voice of the waves and the barking of a dog in the distance were the only sounds which

94

broke the silence of that hour, solemn for one of those men, who was about to lose even the comfort of hope.

Estêvão was the first to speak.

"She loves another, doesn't she?" he asked with a tremulous voice.

"Yes, she does," answered Luis Alves dully.

Estêvão stood up and took a few steps without saying a word, biting the tip of his mustache, stopping abruptly at times, at others revealing with a wild gesture the feelings that thundered in his heart. The pain must have been great, but its manifestation now wasn't the same as that which the reader observed when, two years before, he went to confide to his friend the discouragement Guiomar had given him.

"It seems to me I should have guessed just that," he said finally, stopping in front of Luis Alves. "The desire I felt to come here at this hour without being sure I would find you, was a blessing of destiny. I should have expected it. What a life mine has been, Luis! I clung on, I don't even know why, to the hope of being loved by her, of winning her over by means of pity, remorse, or through whatever other motive possible—the motive mattered little. The main thing was that she pay me in tenderness and love for all the pains I suffered, all the tears I swallowed in silence . . . which made me feel happy, as happy as a wretch can be, as *I* could be, who was born under an evil star. . . . Oh! if you only knew. . . . No, you don't know; neither does she; no one knows nor will ever know what I have suffered, all I have. . . ."

He interrupted himself. Two tears, squeezed from the bottom of his heart, sprang from his eyes and ran down his cheeks rapidly to lose themselves among the few thin hairs of his beard. Feeling that other tears might come, he went and sat down on a sofa with his back turned to Luis Alves. Others did come, because his heart still had them for such supreme pains; but they ran down silently, without a whimper, without even one complaint.

Luis Alves had gotten up and gone to the window. His spirit, despite its coldness and quietness, now seemed to be a little restless. It wasn't pain; and I'm not sure that I could call it remorse. Perhaps discomfort, and commiseration. His heart was capable of affection; but as was pointed out in the first chapter, he knew how to govern and moderate it, and guide it to serve his own purposes. He was neither corrupt nor perverse; neither can it be said, however, that he was loyal and gallant; he was, after all has been said, a coldly ambitious man.

Estêvão was up again and had grabbed his hat.

"Come here," said Luis Alves, pulling his head inside the window and going over where he was. "I can see you are more a man than before. What remains is for you to be completely a man; sweep from your memory and heart all that can remind you. . . ."

"What a cure!" interrupted Estêvão, smiling bitterly. "What else can I do but forget her! But when will I?"

"Sooner perhaps than you think. . . ."

Luis Alves didn't finish; Estêvão had looked at him with an air of astonishment and had sat down again.

"Sooner than I expect!" he exclaimed. "You don't have a heart; you don't even have insight or memory. Can't you see, can't you feel, that this love is the blood of my blood and the life of my life? Forget her! It would be well if I could, but my ill-fated destiny tears even that hope from me. Surely this incessant inner misery will follow me to my death. . . ."

This time it was Luis Alves who paced the floor. In his mind an idea was being conceived, and he was examining it to decide whether he might put it into action then and there. It was to tell Estêvão everything. He would find it out later anyway; it was best that he find out right away and from him. At the same time Luis was thinking about the fine sentiments of the boy; the pain would certainly become intense when he found out whom Guiomar preferred. The heart that could forgive a stranger would condemn a friend.

Estêvão, leaning back, his eyes on the ceiling, seemed lost in thought; but it only seemed that way, because he wasn't thinking, he was evoking old memories, calling to mind the gentle picture of Guiomar; he felt the dominance of her beautiful brown eyes, he could hear her sweet and velvet voice echoing through his heart. He wasn't only evoking, he was also creating; with his imagination he was envisioning the happiness the girl could give him if she would choose him from among all others, if the two were to join their destinies. He could imagine her close to him; he would place his arm around her waist, fill her hair with kisses, all of this in the midst of a panorama unique on earth, where the abundance of nature would increase in contact with that pure, chaste, and eternal sentiment. It is not I speaking, reader; I am simply and faithfully transcribing the lover's thoughts; I am recording on this piece of paper the flights he was making into airy space, the only venture permitted him.

In the midst of these visions, Luís Alves awakened him.

"You are right to feel," said the latter. "But don't waste your heart, for greater surprises await you in life. . . . In any case, let me tell you that you have no reason to condemn—"

"Am I condemning someone?"

"There is in love a germ of hatred which can develop later. You may come to accuse her of not loving you; when you do that, remember that the movements of the heart are not a matter of will. It's not her fault if another awakened love within her."

"Ah! She entrusted you with her defense!"

Luís Alves smiled; he was expecting to be reprimanded.

"No, she didn't entrust me with her defense," he said. "I am taking it into my own hands. After all, what am I defending except nature, reason, and the logic of feelings, as hard and inflexible as any other kind of logic? Behind your words is a feeling of egotism. . . ."

"Love is nothing but that," answered Estêvão, smiling himself. "Do you expect me, on top of everything, to thank her for my desperation? Do you expect me to shake the hand of the man who knew how to win her over?"

Luís Alves bit the tip of his tongue and went over to the window. When he was about to turn back in, he heard a slight noise at the window below, the first window of the baroness' house; Luis Alves took another step. He saw no one; all he saw was the tip of a fleeting dress, and something that fell at his feet; he bent over to pick it up. It was a large piece of paper, wrapped around another small sheet of paper, doubled four times in order to make it heavier. Luis Alves moved up to the light and read rapidly what was written there. He read it, stuck the paper in his pocket, and walked over to the window. No one; the baroness' house was asleep.

When he turned back inside, Estêvão had gotten up. He had seen the paper fall and Luis Alves pick it up and read it. He had no idea what was going on, but his look asked for an explanation.

Luis Alves went straight to the finish.

"Estêvão," he said, "you are going to know the whole truth; I couldn't keep from you what has happened; and it probably wouldn't be wise for you to hear it from another's lips. Guiomar could have loved you, you were worthy of her and she worthy of you; but nature didn't make you for each other. You are two excellent souls who would be unhappy together. Who is to blame here? But if nature explains her feelings, she also explains those of a third party—I. You trusted me with the pains and hopes of your heart; in doing so, you experienced my friendship and the profound esteem I have always felt for you. But neither you nor I were expecting me to enter the picture; I also have a heart and the distinctions of beauty also speak to my soul. I couldn't look at her with cold eyes. Love blinded me; in my happiness of loving and being loved, please believe that I am somewhat unhappy because of your tears, your long and cruel suffering, which I am aware of and deplore. Mine is a frank confession; I'm not speaking to you of repentance, because these are acts of my heart and not of my conscience, which is pure and honorable. And after this faithful exposition, I believe you will regret along with me the fact that fate or bad luck brought the three of us together; but surely you won't accuse me or refuse me your old esteem. I'm speaking only of esteem; our friendship, I believe, can't be the same. But you will respect, I hope, my character. As for my part, neither one of these perishes; I know your worth. I don't know where the wave of destiny will cast us tomorrow. For the last time, however, I hope that you will shake your friend's hand."

Luis Alves had concluded by extending his hand to him. Estêvão looked at him but didn't say one word, didn't make one gesture; he walked to the door and left.

"Estêvão!" Luis Alves cried.

But the only answer he got was the sound of feet descending, and shortly after, that of the carriage that rolled along quietly on the damp gravel of the beach.

Luis Alves shrugged his shoulders drily; he approached the light and read the writing.

17 ⁄ The Letter

He didn't have to reread the paper to understand it; but eyes in love take delight in love letters. The paper contained only the following—*Ask for my hand*—written in the center of the page, in a fine, elegant, and feminine handwriting. Luis Alves looked at the note for a while, first as a man in love, then as a mere observer. The handwriting wasn't shaky, but seemed to have been cast upon the paper in a moment of agitation.

From this observation Luis Alves passed on to a very natural reflection. That note, hardly advisable in any other circumstances, was justified by reason of the declaration he himself had made to the girl a few days before, when he asked that she get to know him first and that on the day she found him worthy of being her husband he would hear her and follow her. But if this was the case with relation to the note, it wasn't with relation to the hour.

99

What motive would cause the girl to throw him that decisive note through the window at midnight, a note that was eloquent even in the sobriety with which she had written it?

Luis Alves concluded that there was some urgent reason, and that therefore it was necessary to respond to the occasion as the occasion demanded. As for the reason itself, he wasn't able to puzzle it out. The fact of Jorge's courtship of Guiomar, otherwise obvious, did occur to him, but he was ignorant of the related circumstances, and wasn't able to go on from there.

I won't say that Luis Alves spent the night digging deep in the area of vague conjectures. He wasn't the type of man to waste time on useless things; and nothing was more useless to him on that occasion than trying to explain what to him could have no explanation. What he decided to do was obey the girl's request, to ask for her without hesitation or preamble. But if the case didn't produce insomnia in him, neither did it fail to keep him up beyond the usual hour, as would be expected on that solemn occasion, especially since it had to do with a creature who in those days was the envy and coveted prize of many an eye. Luis Alves was not like Estêvão, a lovable daydreamer; he didn't feed on imagination and illusion, nourishment which produces little or nothing; but he pondered a while, he engrossed himself for an hour in the ideal contemplation of the woman he had known how to choose. He grew sleepy and the illusion blended itself with the dream.

Would Guiomar be sleeping as relaxed as he? She was; the night, however, had been much more troubled and bitter for her, as would be expected after Jorge's declaration and her godmother's insinuations.

The girl had retired to her room immediately following the declaration. The members of the household were unable to read anything in her face, except the sudden paleness and the blush that followed it; but, as soon as she was alone, she gave full vent to the feelings which, up to that moment, she had been able to contain.

The first of these was resentment; Guiomar felt humiliated

100

with that declaration, sprung that way like a trap and so suddenly in order to wrench from her a consent her heart and spirit rejected. No consultation, no previous authorization; it seemed to her that she was being treated as an absolutely passive entity, without either free will or choice, destined to satisfy alien whims. Her godmother's words contradicted this supposition; but the information she had on the baroness' resolution about this business greatly diminished the value of such words. If it was to be an "all absorbing interest," as Mrs. Oswald had said, they wanted to camouflage it with appearances of moderation, and the time they were leaving her to reflect about it was actually intended for her to consider the necessity of paying back the favors she had received.

Don't condemn her for having made these reflections—her eyes flashing and her lips cold with wrath—as soon as she got back to her room. They were natural; first, because she supposed that her marriage to Jorge had been planned and would be realized whatever the circumstances; then, because her soul was vain; it wasn't forgetting the favors received, but she had hoped that they wouldn't call her attention to them by violent means . . . to do that was the same thing as throwing them in her face.

"No!" the girl finally muttered. "To force me, to reduce me to the condition of a simple servant, that never!"

But this wrath waned, and her heart won out in the end. Guiomar recalled the baroness' constant kindness toward her, the solicitude with which she satisfied her smallest wishes, which were as commands in that house, and she couldn't reconcile such great love with the supposed violence she wanted to do her. It wasn't long before Guiomar had repented the incoherent words that had escaped her and the evil sentiments she had attributed to the baroness' heart. She crossed her hands on her bosom and lifted her thoughts to heaven, as though asking forgiveness. Guiomar, in the midst of life's seductions, which were to her so many and which so completely blinded her, had not lost her religious feeling, nor had she forgotten what her mother's native and pure faith had taught her.

The wrath had ended, but then came the fight between gratitude and love, between the fiancé, which her godmother's affection proposed as ideal and the one her own heart had chosen. She dared neither to destroy the baroness' hopes nor sacrifice her own, and it was necessary that she do one of the two on that solemn occasion. She struggled long and painfully with her feelings and thoughts; but if such a duel could burn in her soul, the result was not to be doubted. Will and ambition, when they truly dominate, can struggle with other feelings, but they are sure to win, because they are the weapons of the strong, and victory belongs to the strong. Guiomar had to decide between one of two men that were to determine her destiny; she chose the one that spoke to her heart.

The girl, however, couldn't delay the answer, nor evade it; it was not wise to prolong the fight and the uncertainty. When she felt this, a decisive idea occurred to her, that of confessing everything to her godmother. She hesitated, however, between doing it herself and doing it through Luis Alves, whose words she had preserved in her memory. She preferred this last means; but it wasn't enough to prefer it, it was necessary to put it into effect, and to do that she had only two means at her disposal: to write or speak to him. The second of these alternatives could not be soon, and there was the possibility of not finding a proper occasion; she adopted the first, then hesitated. The letter could be sent by a servant, but Guiomar's mind was in such turmoil that she rejected such intervention. The window was open; from there she saw a light in Luis Alves' living room and the young man's shadow, walking back and forth. It was then that the idea occurred to her which she put into effect, as was related in the previous chapter.

Such is the story of those words written rapidly on a sheet of paper. In spite of Luis Alves' proposal and the circumstances the girl found herself in, the reader will easily understand that she didn't write it without struggling with herself, without vacillating between unwillingness and necessity. Finally the scruples were defeated, which is so often their destiny, and it ought to be said that they are never defeated without cost, because they speak, they reason, they fight hard to win; but it is common to pass over them. No sooner had the girl thrown the letter, however, than she regretted having done it; her dignity felt remorse, her conscience almost accused her of a vile act. It was too late; the letter had reached its destination.

The following morning the baroness awakened happier than usual. She thought she had seen in Guiomar, the night before, something which seemed to be only a natural entanglement of the situation. Guiomar had risen late; it was a rainy morning and her godmother didn't take her walk. The girl went to kiss her hand and cheek, as she customarily did, and receive the maternal kiss. Her face seemed tired, but a veil of affected happiness hid a natural expression, like that of a mannikin, so that the baroness, no great reader of countenances, wasn't able to discern in that particular one the truth of its imposture. I say imposture; nevertheless one should understand it to be honest and upright, because the girl's intent was no more than not to make her godmother unhappy, and to avoid any anticipated worry.

"Did my queen of England sleep well?" asked Mrs. Oswald, placing her hands on Guiomar's shoulders in a familiar way.

"Your queen of England has no crown," answered Guiomar with a constrained smile.

Around midday the baroness received a letter from Luis Alves. She opened it and read it. The lawyer was asking her for Guiomar's hand. A few lines, courteous, simple, natural, written by one who seemed master of the situation.

"Mrs. Oswald," said the baroness to her companion who was in the same room. "Read this."

The Englishwoman obeyed.

"This doesn't mean anything," she observed after a few moments. "It's just another suitor; we must realize, however, that there are many of them, and if the others don't write you letters like these, it's because they are less bold. Does Madame Baroness think the eyes of her goddaughter are innocent?" continued the Englishwoman, smiling. "I believe they are heavy with guilt and that there are many victims. . . ."

"But don't you see, Mrs. Oswald," interrupted the baroness, "that this man sounds as if he's been authorized?"

Mrs. Oswald grew quiet, as though reflecting. Soon afterward she brought forth a series of arguments and considerations, which if not serious in substance, could not have been better stated—at least, in the manner in which she stated them, some in seriously British fashion—even by a member of the House of Commons. Every part of her being gave an impression of lively and irrefutable argument. There was in her hair, a mixture of blonde and white, all the rigidity of a syllogism; each nostril looked like the horn of a dilemma. The conclusion of it all was that nothing was lost, and that Jorge's happiness was something not only possible but even probable, once the baroness had showed—and this was essential—a certain resolve, which was very useful and even indispensable under the circumstances. Mrs. Oswald offered to summon the girl immediately.

"Well, go, go," said the baroness.

The Englishwoman left and went after Guiomar. When she saw her from a distance she forced a smile, and Guiomar, seeing her smile, experienced something like an internal feeling of repulsion.

"I've come to get you," said Mrs. Oswald, "for something you're far from imagining."

Guiomar questioned her with her eyes.

"To marry!"

"Marry!" exclaimed Guiomar, without understanding the messenger's intent.

"Nothing less," the former replied. "You're surprised, aren't you? So am I; and your godmother as well. But someone has had the bad taste to fall in love with your beautiful eyes, and the effrontery to come and ask for you as though asking for the stars in heaven. . . ."

Guiomar understood what it was about. She looked disdainfully at the Englishwoman, and said in an annoyed and curt tone:

"But finish, Mrs. Oswald."

"Madame Baroness has sent for you."

Guiomar prepared to meet her godmother; Mrs. Oswald made her stop for a moment, and in the most ingratiating voice she possessed, she said:

"All the happiness of this house is in your hands."

18 ' The Choice

Mrs. Oswald had said too much. The baroness had not told her to tell her goddaughter why she was being called. As it turned out, however, that was not the only indiscretion. Mrs. Oswald, instead of stepping out of the way and leaving the discussion of the subject to Guiomar and the baroness, yielded to curiosity and accompanied the girl.

The baroness was seated between two windows with the letter open in her hands, so intent in rereading it that she didn't hear the footsteps of Guiomar and Mrs. Oswald.

"Did my godmother call me?" Guiomar asked, stopping in front of her.

The baroness lifted her head.

"Ah! It's true; yes; I called you. Sit down right here."

Guiomar pulled over the nearest chair and sat near the baroness. The latter, meanwhile, had folded the letter slowly, her eyes on the floor, as though looking for a place to begin. When she raised them, she saw the Englishwoman. She was going to speak but she held back a moment. The affection she had for her didn't hinder her from finding Mrs. Oswald's presence undesirable on such an occasion. She waited a few moments, but as the Englishwoman seemed to be entirely unaware of it, she said:

"Mrs. Oswald, go see if the birds have been fed."

The Englishwoman perceived that "the birds," in this case, was purely a metaphor, and that all the baroness had in mind was to ask her, as charmingly as possible, to leave. Nonetheless, she didn't let her feeling show.

"It seems to me they haven't," she said. "I'll go see about it right now."

"Listen," said the baroness, when she was already on her way, "pull those doors to for me and give orders that we are not to be disturbed."

The Englishwoman obeyed and left. No one was able to see the wry face she made as she left, and nothing was lost by it.

The two remained alone.

"Sit down over here, Guiomar," said the baroness, pointing to a little bench that was at her feet.

Guiomar left the chair and came over to sit on the bench, resting her arms lovingly on her godmother's knees. The latter placed her hands on Guiomar's head and remained that way a long time without speaking, in eloquent silence in which only the heart spoke. Both were distraught; Guiomar, in the midst of a sigh, whispered only this sweet name:

"Mother!"

It was the first time she had called her that, and it touched the baroness' soul so deeply that her answer was to cover her with kisses.

"Yes, your mother," said the baroness. "The one who gave you life couldn't love you more than I. You possess the soul and tenderness of the daughter heaven took from me, and if all mothers who lose their children could find substitutes in the same way, the most cruel of all pains in the world would disappear. . . ."

Guiomar's answer was to squeeze her hands and kiss them. There followed a pause, in which emotion disappeared little by little, and the baroness looked at Luis Alves' letter, which had been crumpled by Guiomar's movements.

"Guiomar," she asked, finally, "have you thought about last night's proposal yet?"

106

The girl had expected her to talk about Luis Alves' proposal; the baroness' question disconcerted her a little. Her mind, however, was clear and astute; her answer was another question.

"Should one night be enough to decide about the rest of one's life?"

"You're right, dear; but it was a natural question coming from a person who wants to see a wish materialize. Jorge asked for your hand in marriage. Do you realize he's an excellent fellow?"

"Excellent," answered the girl.

"A good soul," continued the baroness, "and a distinguished young man. He seems to like you very much, according to what he said yesterday, don't you think? That's natural; I would only be surprised if there weren't many others in love with you."

The baroness stopped; Guiomar was playing with the embroidery of her sleeve without daring to raise her eyes.

"You must know," continued the baroness, "that I should be very happy to see this marriage take place; I am convinced it would make you happy, and him also, at least insofar as one is able to judge from present circumstances. . . . What does your heart say?"

And since Guiomar didn't answer readily:

"Ah! I was forgetting what you told me just a while ago. One night isn't enough to decide about the rest of your life. Well; you'll hear two more things from me. The first is that . . . read this letter yourself."

The baroness gave Guiomar the letter, who opened it and read the request that Luis Alves was making for her hand. As she ran over the few written lines with her eyes, her godmother seemed to be watching her closely as if trying to read in her face the impression the request made, whether surprise or satisfaction. Neither surprise nor satisfaction were apparent; Guiomar read the letter and returned it to her godmother.

"Did you read it? That's the first thing I wanted to tell you. Dr. Luis Alves is asking for your hand in marriage; you must choose between him and Jorge. The second thing is that, of the two suitors, Jorge is the one my heart prefers; but I am not the one getting married; you are; choose with complete freedom the one who speaks to your heart."

Guiomar straightened and looked directly at her godmother, with such signs of surprise in her face that the latter could not keep from asking her:

"What's the matter?"

The girl didn't answer; I mean she didn't answer with her lips; she grabbed her godmother's hand and squeezed it between her own, and kept looking at her as if reflecting. The expression on her face had changed from astonishment to satisfaction and from this to something that looked like indignation and aversion at the same time.

"Oh! Mother!" exclaimed Guiomar. "Why didn't our hearts understand each other from the beginning? It was unfortunate to have misgivings come between us. If I could have foreseen the feeling you've just expressed, I wouldn't have suffered half of what I have been made to suffer for many days. . . ."

"Suffer?"

"Yes, suffer! Nothing less. But let's leave this aside. It was your heart that spoke and mine that heard; I can now tell you frankly what I feel, without fear of hurting you."

She didn't have to say any more; the choice she was going to make was already indicated, at least. The baroness understood that and closed her eyes, sighing. Her goddaughter heard her sigh and noticed her sudden sadness; she regretted having gone so far.

"I understand," answered the baroness. "You mean to say that of the two suitors, you choose Dr. Luis Alves."

The girl remained silent; her godmother was looking at her with an anxious expression which troubled her.

"Speak," repeated the baroness.

"I choose . . . Jorge," sighed Guiomar after a few instants.

The baroness trembled.

"Are you serious? I don't believe it; that's not the feeling of your heart. One can see it's not. You want to fool me and yourself as well. I can tell you don't love him; you never loved

108

him. But you love the other, don't you? What does that matter? You aren't giving me the pleasure I would have if. . . . What does it matter, if you will be happy? Your happiness is more important than my likes and dislikes. It was a dream of mine; I wished it with all my strength; I would have done everything I could to achieve it; but a heart cannot be forced—especially a heart like yours! You choose the other one? Well, you shall marry him."

The reader can see that the awaited word, the word the girl felt come from her heart to her lips and try to part them, that it was not she who pronounced it but her godmother; and if you read what preceded attentively you will see that it was just that that she wanted. But why did Jorge's name pass her lips? The girl didn't want to deceive the baroness but to convey unfaithfully the voice of her heart in order that her godmother would, on her own, compare the translation against the original. There was in this a bit of the circuitous, a bit of tactic, of affectation, I'm almost saying of hypocrisy, if you don't misunderstand my use of the term. There was, but this itself will tell you that this Guiomar, without forfeiting the excellencies of her heart, was of the ordinary clay that God made our seldom sincere humanity, and will tell you that in spite of her tender years, she already knew that the appearance of a sacrifice is ofttimes worth more than the sacrifice itself.

The baroness had finished talking. The happiness on Guiomar's face confirmed the baroness' first impression, and if the choice were contrary to the one she wished for, her goddaughter's pleasure repaid her for everything she was going to lose. Such was that mother's good soul, good, dedicated, and generous.

"O Mother! Thank you!" the girl exclaimed. "But won't you hate me?"

"Pshaw!" exclaimed the baroness in a reprimanding tone.

And she pulled Guiomar close and hugged her lovingly. Guiomar responded to the gesture and the two merged their intimate happiness and sincere affections.

Mrs. Oswald saw them soon afterwards, smiling and in

agreement. It was easy to see which of the two suitors had won; Guiomar was not likely to have received with such good spirits the baroness' nephew. It was all finished; perhaps she herself had suffered in that last encounter. The baroness had asked Guiomar to explain to her what suffering she was referring to, but the girl preferred to say nothing, not only not to afflict her godmother, but also so as not to lend an appearance of rivalry to the situation between herself and Mrs. Oswald.

The choice was made, the consent given. The baroness answered the happy suitor that same afternoon. Estêvão would have manifested loudly all the happiness that such an answer would have brought him; his impassioned and exuberant soul would have told God and men of that immense good fortune. Luis Alves locked up within himself the pleasure, otherwise great; he thought about the girl and about the future for a few instants, but spoke to no one of them.

The baroness wrote her nephew the same day, giving him Guiomar's answer. The reader will not find it difficult to believe that Jorge's heart didn't feel the blow deeply, but he did feel something. He didn't go to his aunt's house that night; he didn't go the next night either; on the third night he descended the stairs; on the fourth he headed out to Botafogo.

"Everything is finished," his aunt told him, truly sorrowful.

"Finished!" sighed Jorge.

"Now it is necessary to be brave; I hope you will be a man."

"Oh! I'll be a man!" sighed Jorge again.

And two sighs wrenched from the bosom of such a serious man had forcibly to be two very serious ones, as the reader can easily believe.

Actually, the young man's countenance showed neither despondency nor distress; it was not creased by even the slightest vestige of an ill-slept night—even less so, of dried tears. It wasn't a happy face, but grave and austere, as it always was, in contrast with the youthful stiffness of his mustache.

The baroness imagined, nevertheless, that her nephew's pain

must have really hurt him; and she squeezed his hands with tenderness and said yet a few words of encouragement to him.

One can imagine what the first meeting between Jorge and Guiomar was like. The girl was serene, perhaps smiling, and even compassionate. If she had had to marry him, she would probably have hated him; now she had already forgiven him for his love. Jorge, for his part, couldn't avoid being a bit shaken, partly emotion, partly embarrassment—the embarrassment, however, being greater than the emotion. Upon his lips there settled one of those smiles in which the penetrating eye or picturesque imagination of the public would discover a yellow hue. If the look had been any other, it is likely that she would have at least continued to respect him. But that smile truly characterized him in the mind of Guiomar.

On the first occasion which offered itself, Jorge unfolded himself to Mrs. Oswald.

"Everything has been lost," he sighed.

The Englishwoman didn't answer.

"Everything has been lost," the baroness' nephew said finally, "maybe because of you."

"Me?" asked Mrs. Oswald.

"You."

"But . . ."

Jorge hesitated for a moment.

"You didn't show enough enthusiasm," he said then.

"What do you want?" asked Mrs. Oswald. "A heart cannot be dominated, nor is there any means of imposing a feeling upon it. Guiomar is a saintly creature, she really loves your rival; is there anything more just than for them to marry each other?"

"So . . ."

"So it was right to do everything possible in the assumption that she didn't love another, but once it was known that she does love. . . ."

Luis Alves, on the night of the day in which he received the letter, went to the baroness' house, where he was received with the best of her smiles. Guiomar's happiness made her completely happy; no anger or resentment, as Mrs. Oswald had said. From the moment the baroness' sincerity intervened, the entire castle of letters had fallen to the ground.

Conclusion

The wedding date having been set for two months thereafter, the entire interval was spent by the couple in that delectable type of living which is no longer the furtive language of mere courtship, neither yet is it conjugal intimacy, but an intermediate and mutual state in which the hearts can overflow freely into each other. These two had none of Estêvão's ecstatic and romantic love, but they loved sincerely, she even more than he, and one was as happy as the other.

The people who knew them commented in every way and manner about that unexpected affair, and more than one person was most envious of the favor with which heaven had treated Luis Alves. The girl's daintiness and elegance met objection in no one's mind; everyone acknowledged and applauded them, because even the offended silence of rival beauties (if, in effect, there were any) was likewise applause, and of the best kind. As to Guiomar's character, the appreciation of it was diverse; and one day when Luis Alves was relating to her some threads of a conversation he overheard about his bride-to-be, she seemed to reflect for a long while, and finally answered:

"It's no surprise to me that there should be so many different opinions; it is natural, because I never spoke freely of my feelings. In any case, others' opinions matter little to me; I should like to know yours."

"Mine is that you are an angel."

Guiomar made a delicate gesture of irritation, as though not expecting that oft-used compliment, otherwise always new—

because there is none better nor more beautiful in our Christian language. The groom-to-be smiled but said nothing to her, yet he might have said something—at least that which the reader heard him say in one of the preceding chapters.

"If you don't know what I am," continued Guiomar, "I'll tell you myself, so you won't marry me in ignorance, and so you won't accidentally marry a demon, believing that she is an angel. . . ."

"A demon!" exclaimed Luis Alves, laughing.

"No more nor less," she retorted, also laughing. "Please know, then, that I have a mind of my own, but am not much for expressing it; I like for people to guess about me and obey me; I am also a bit naughty, sometimes capricious, and on top of all this, I have a demanding heart. Can you find more defects than this in one bundle?"

Luis Alves answered that they were all excellent qualities, and was about to tell her that there remained yet another, which was the most fundamental of all; he preferred to allude to it after the marriage.

The wedding took place on the appointed date with the proper solemnities. The morning of that day wore a mantle of dense fog, which our winter had placed around its shoulders as if to protect it from the benign rigor of the temperature, a mantle which it shook off soon afterward in order to show itself as it was, a delightful and refreshing Rio morning. It wasn't long before the sun shone squarely on the blue and tranquil waters and the hills where the natural green alternated with the white of human habitations. No wind at all; only a soft and cool breeze, which seemed like the last breath of the already remote night, and which agitated the leaves on the bushes only in certain spots.

The estate that day was the same as on every other day, but Guiomar found a new and better side to it, something like a divine diffusion that gave life to the things around it. All happy souls are pantheistic; it seems to them that God smiles at them from inside the budding flower, from the depths of the water that

113

winds along, murmuring, and even from the unpretentious and wild vines or coarse, stony ground beneath. That was the way Guiomar's soul felt that morning. Never before had the trees, the flowers, the close-cut grass seemed to her more exuberant; her inner feelings absorbed that exterior life in the same way that her lungs drank in the pure morning air.

Amid those sensations common to all people, there were yet those that were hers—hers, who could see the last sunset of her maiden days and could contemplate in anticipation the new dawn, the long and happy day of her fervent ambitions. At this point the wings of the wild leaf shed the costume they had worn in the midst of that vegetation in order to display others, of silk and brocade, and to fly to what heights of human greatness only heaven knows.

Coincidence willed that that morning she wear the same bathrobe in which Estêvão had seen her on the other side of the fence, and she wore at her neck and at her wrists the same pin and the same sapphire buttons. She didn't have the book; but to make up for that missing item, there was another which was the same as on that celebrated morning: there were some eyes that peeked at her lovingly from the other side of the fence. They weren't, however, the same pair; they were her fiancé's eyes which met hers—and the most painful thing is that not even the fence, nor the other accompaniments—nothing—reminded her of the other man, who was about to die because of her. Such is the way with happiness; seldom does it have time for memories of the past.

The baroness seemed no less happy than she that day. From time to time in the distance, the memory of her nephew would appear to her, but no longer was there regret that the union that she had hoped for had not been carried out; the blow to Jorge was so light, and so indifferently did he move about, that the good lady understood that if love had existed, it wasn't great and above all, not lasting; the thought that this might have happened to him after six months of marriage made her thank God for the failure of her plans.

114

Mrs. Oswald also appeared to be happy, perhaps even more so because she had an air of magniloquence, as if wanting to make up for past mistakes. Guiomar could well understand the concealed intent of the effusive manifestations she employed in congratulating her and making over her; but it was no time for rancor or resentment, and she received the Englishwoman's affected courtesies, smiling.

The wedding finally took place. The tears the baroness shed when she saw Guiomar forever united, were the finest jewels she could give her. No mother ever shed them more sincerely; and, let it be said in favor of Guiomar, no daughter ever appreciated them more deeply in her heart.

On the wedding night, anyone who looked toward the sea could see, not far from the groups of curious people attracted by the feasting of a large and grand mansion, the figure of a man sitting on a flagstone he happened to find there. Those who are accustomed to reading novels and have read this narrative from the beginning must immediately suppose that this man must be Estêvão. It was he. Perhaps the reader, under similar circumstances, would have sought refuge in so remote a place that the memory of the past could scarcely haunt him. But Estêvão's soul felt a cruel and singular need, the satisfaction of turning the blade in the wound, something which we might call—the voluptuousness of pain, for lack of a better word. And he went there, to contemplate with the indifferent and idle, that house where happiness and life reigned, at a time when the past and future, off of which he had lived, would be forever buried. The stoic's outlook didn't sustain him; down his thin and pale face ran the final tears, and his heart, gathering up its remaining strength, was throbbing strongly in the recesses of his bosom.

Before him the jubilant mansion shone with all its lights; behind him, the slow and melancholic wave broke, and the far end of the cove could be seen, dark and sad. The mood of the place served the plan he had conceived, which was no less than to kill himself right there when it got to the point he could no longer stand the pain, a kind of final vengeance he would take upon those who were making him suffer so much, complicating their happiness with remorse.

But this plan couldn't materialize, for the simple reason that it was just another illusion, which dissipated itself like the others. His indecision denied him this last ambition. His eyes could look at death as they could at fortune; but he lacked the means by which to travel to it. He remained there, then, until the end; and instead of diving into the water and into nothingness as he had planned, he returned sadly home, stumbling like a drunkard, leaving there behind him his entire youth, because what he was taking with him was something discolored and dry, sterile and dead. The years went by, and as they moved along, Estêvão sank into the vast and dark sea of the anonymous masses. The name which didn't pass from the memory of his friends died right there, when fate took him away from them. Whether he is still vegetating in some corner of the capital, or whether he wound up in some village of the interior, is not known.

Destiny shouldn't have lied nor did it lie to Luis Alves' ambition. Guiomar was right; here was a strong man. A month after their marriage, as they were talking about those things newlyweds talk about, namely themselves, and recalling the brief period of courtship, Guiomar confessed to her husband that on that occasion, she had recognized in him all the power of his will.

"I saw that you were a man with a resolute mind," said the girl to Luis Alves who, seated, was listening to her.

"Resolute and ambitious," added Luis Alves, smiling. "You must have perceived that I am one and the other as well."

"Ambition is no defect."

"On the contrary, it is a virtue; I feel that I have it and that I am sure to make it succeed. I am not counting only on my youth and moral strength; I am depending on you also; you will be a new source of strength to me."

"Oh, I hope so!" exclaimed Guiomar.

And in a mischievous manner, she continued:

116

"But what will you give me in return? a seat in the Chamber of Deputies? a position as minister?"

"The prestige of my name," he answered.

Guiomar, who was standing before him, her hands locked in his, let herself slide slowly down upon her husband's knees, and the two ambitions exchanged an affectionate kiss. Both settled down as if that glove had been made for that hand.

DESIGN BY JONATHAN GREENE
PRINTED & BOUND BY KINGSPORT PRESS